D0296576

This book should be returned to any branch of the
Lancashire County Library on or before the date shown

Dear Reader

There are times in life when every person comes face to face with his or her own mortality. As I brainstormed Greg and Hannah's story I thought about people who overcome incredible challenges, and how they seem to relish life with an intensity others can only dream of. I wanted Hannah's character to have this same passion as someone who's faced down a life-threatening illness and made a conscious decision to live every moment to its fullest. Even if some of those moments have unexpected consequences...

Thank you for joining Greg and Hannah as they experience the joy and heartbreak of working in a difficult field. Their dedication to their patients and to each other helps them rise to meet each new challenge. Best of all, this special couple finds love along the way.

I hope you enjoy reading about their journey as much as I enjoyed writing about it!

Sincerely

Tina Beckett

"How's your back?"

She wiggled the upper part of her body back and forth to feel it out, then realized she'd just done a quick shimmy against his thorax.

"Can't feel a thing."

The hand at her back tightened. "Can't you?"

Um, yeah... And it wasn't good. Because she was suddenly aware of every inch of male flesh pressed against her. Muscular chest, firm abs, taut thighs, and…

No, it couldn't be. She licked her lips, telling herself to pull back now before he realized that *she* realized that *he* was…

He was...

Yes. He *was*.

The sound of his breath hissing in through his teeth met her ears.

Okay. Now he knew that she knew.

She slowly lifted her head and met eyes that were sizzling with something she hadn't seen in a very long time in a man. Especially not directed at her.

Desire.

Steaming. Naked. Toe-curling need.

ONE NIGHT THAT CHANGED EVERYTHING

BY
TINA BECKETT

MILLS
BOON

First published in Great Britain 2012
by Mills & Boon, an imprint of Harlequin (UK) Limited.
Large Print edition 2013
Harlequin (UK) Limited, Eton House,
18-24 Paradise Road, Richmond, Surrey TW9 1SR

© Tina Beckett 2012

ISBN: 978 0 263 23112 0   118232093

Printed and bound in Great Britain
by CPI Antony Rowe, Chippenham, Wiltshire

Born to a family that was always on the move, **Tina Beckett** learned to pack a suitcase almost before she knew how to tie her shoes. Fortunately she met a man who also loved to travel, and she snapped him right up. Married for over twenty years, Tina has three wonderful children and has lived in gorgeous places such as Portugal and Brazil.

Living where English reading material is difficult to find has its drawbacks, however. Tina had to come up with creative ways to satisfy her love for romance novels, so she picked up her pen and tried writing one. After her tenth book she realised she was hooked. She was officially a writer.

A three-times Golden Heart finalist, and fluent in Portuguese, Tina now divides her time between the United States and Brazil. She loves to use exotic locales as the backdrop for many of her stories. When she's not writing you can find her either on horseback or soldering stained glass panels for her home.

Tina loves to hear from readers. You can contact her through her website or 'friend' her on Facebook.

Recent titles by the same author:

THE MAN WHO WOULDN'T MARRY
DOCTOR'S MILE-HIGH FLING
DOCTOR'S GUIDE TO DATING IN THE JUNGLE

These books are also available in eBook format from www.millsandboon.co.uk

For those who embrace life.

CHAPTER ONE

"MRS. BROOKSTONE went under hospice care last night."

The words met Hannah Lassiter the second she pushed through the glass doors of the Alaska Valley Oncology Center. She glanced at her watch, her shoulders slumping. Only seven-thirty, but she had no doubt her boss was already here. Had already heard the news. "Oh, no. Where is he?"

She didn't really need to ask. Dr. Gregory Mason would be holed up in his office until his first appointment. Dedicated to providing the best care possible, news like this—even when it was expected—had the power to bring Dr. Mason's world crashing to a halt for an hour or two. At least until he rose from his chair, closed the door on this particular compartment in his head and got back to work. It was eerie, really, how he could seemingly wall off certain portions of his brain at will.

The receptionist answered her question with a jerk of her thumb.

Hannah sighed. "When's his first patient due in?"

"Martha Brookstone *was* his first patient. We've cancelled the appointment."

"Don't put anyone else in her slot, okay? I'll check on him."

Easier said than done. Her employer, a brilliant doctor, insisted on doing much of the scheduling himself, which was a nightmare for his staff, who had to scramble to keep up with him.

Yet every single person in that office had benefitted from his indefatigable nature, including Hannah herself.

A year in remission and counting. She'd never even seen it coming. A routine checkup two years ago had uncovered enlarged lymph nodes.

Cancer.

She'd moved from her position at a tiny clinic in the Aleutian Islands to Anchorage for treatment. Dr. Mason had convinced her to stay on as one of his staff afterward.

Today, of all days, though, she was going to have a tough time keeping her mind on her job. She'd had her own doctor's appointment yesterday. Her chance at a new beginning.

Rounding the U-shaped receptionist desk to

check the printed schedule, she frowned. The list stretched well into the evening. Seven o'clock. And the word *hospital* was penciled in after the last appointment.

How did he do it?

While some doctors crammed in as many patients as possible, Dr. Mason worked long, hard hours but his patients were spread out, most covering an entire half-hour block, some up to an hour—especially the newly diagnosed. She ran a finger down the list. Three new cases. Blowing out a breath that fluffed her bangs off her forehead, she again wondered why she'd agreed to work for a doctor who represented every fear she'd ever held.

Except for today. Even with the sad news about Martha still floating in the air, this was one day she'd force herself to flatten the past and let the hope of a shining future take hold and grow into something wonderful. Just as she hoped that little blast of sperm she'd received yesterday would grow and multiply.

Too bad that blast had been from the end of a syringe. But it was the only kind of action she was likely to get. Especially with the schedule she'd been keeping lately. It was almost as bad as her boss's.

And if the little swimmers hit their mark, she'd have to talk to Dr. Mason about cutting back and possibly finding a replacement as her time got near.

A lot depended on the damage the chemo had done to her eggs. Dr. Mason had put her on a lighter regimen in an effort to preserve her fertility, but even so, she'd banked some of her eggs beforehand, just in case. But she'd decided to start with the easiest option—artificial insemination— and work her way toward the hardest and most expensive procedures. If those all failed, adoption was always an option.

Going to the coffee carafe they kept in the far corner of the office, she poured two cups, one for herself and one for Dr. Mason, who'd probably already let his first cup go stone cold.

"Wish me luck," she said to Stella, who was already busy fielding calls for the nurse who'd arrive soon. The receptionist gave her a thumbs-up sign and went back to writing on the neon green notepad in front of her. The only way she could keep track of things, she'd said.

Stella buzzed her in, and Hannah used her shoulder to push through the metal door that led to a short corridor of exam rooms, at the end of which lay Dr. Mason's cramped office. She didn't know why she bothered going back to see him. He would emerge when he was ready and not a second before.

His door was closed, but since when had she let something like that stop her? Um…never.

Using her elbow to push down the stainless-steel lever, she waited for the click that would allow her to ease it open. Lucky for her, the thing wasn't locked. Kicking it repeatedly wouldn't be the most dignified way of letting him know she was there.

He sat behind an ornately carved mahogany desk, forehead resting on steepled fingers, eyes closed. He didn't bother looking up. "Don't you ever knock?"

His low voice was gruff, and she had to strain to hear it. The sound pulled at her heartstrings, but she couldn't let him know it. They'd played this little dance several times since he'd hired her. No, even before that. The day he'd declared her to be in remission she'd impulsively thrown her arms around his neck and hugged him tight, thanking him. He'd stiffened for a second or two before sliding warm hands across her back and returning the hug. Just as quickly he'd moved away, not quite meeting her eyes during the rest of the appointment.

None of the other staff dared come into his "lair"—as they called it—without an invitation. But Hannah had been raised in a house with five boys. Impulse control and subtlety were not on the menu. Neither were privacy and quiet. And the last thing Dr. Mason needed right now was to sit here alone and brood.

"My hands are full. Besides, would you have let me in?"

His head came up, twin indentations from his fingertips marring the broad surface of his forehead.

How long had he been sitting like that?

"What do you think?" Deep brown eyes met hers. Eyes that had been filled with compassion when he'd treated her Hodgkin's disease were now glittering with annoyance.

"I brought a peace offering." She set both the cups of coffee on his desk, spying a matching paper cup off to the side. It was still full, but when she touched the side of it…

Yep. Icy cold, just as she'd suspected.

Carrying it into the tiny restroom attached to his office, she dumped the contents into the sink, rinsed out the dregs, then threw the cup into the wastebasket.

She joined him again, taking her own cup and sliding into one of the twin chairs on the other side of his desk.

Dr. Mason groaned. Out loud, which made her smile.

"I'll drink it, I promise."

"You're right. You will." She crossed her legs and took a sip of her own coffee. Waiting.

"Damn it, Hannah. You're not my mother."

No, she wasn't. But she was grateful for everything he'd done for her, and this was the only way she could think of to return the favor. It was all he'd allow. And, grudgingly or not, he usually let her have her way.

Right on cue, he picked up the cup and took a sip.

"Stella told me about Mrs. Brookstone. I'm sorry."

He nodded.

Hannah knew the recommendation not to continue chemotherapy had been an agonizing one for

Dr. Mason. He never made those kinds of decisions lightly, which was why he was in here, probably going over each step of his patient's treatment with a fine-toothed comb, wondering if he could have done something differently.

"She's seventy-five, and the cancer had already spread to her lungs by the time her general practitioner diagnosed her."

His eyes closed for a second before sending her a glare. "I've read the chart."

Many times, if she knew him.

"Yes, you read it. But did you accept it?"

A muscle worked in his jaw. "I'll never accept no hope as a diagnosis."

Her heart squeezed at the tightness behind the words. She wasn't saying he should just write the most serious cases off. "That's what makes you the perfect man for this job."

"I sometimes wonder."

She set her coffee on the edge of the desk and leaned forward. "You need to cut back on your schedule. Take some time off just for yourself. You're already on the road to burnout as it is."

His brows went up. "I've been doing this job for ten years. I think I know my own limitations."

"When was the last time you took a vacation?"

She held up a hand before he could answer. "A real one. One that doesn't involve a medical conference or giving some type of lecture."

"You mean like the one you're giving me right now?"

Her face heated. Okay, so he had her there. "Sorry."

He picked up a pen and twirled it, giving her a chance to study him. Dark hair, conservatively cropped, lay thick against his head. Not a hint of grey yet. His broad shoulders were strong and imposing, despite the slight stoop from spending hours bent over operating tables and examining patients. She knew those shoulders led to narrow hips, which were now safely hidden on the other side of the desk.

The fingers that gripped the pen were long and delicate, nimble enough to separate healthy tissue from diseased. She gulped, remembering the gentle way they'd touched the bare skin of her midriff as he'd drawn a permanent marker across the vulnerable surface in preparation for taking a biopsy of one of her thoracic nodes. The way her abdominal muscles had rippled at the contact. Even through the thin latex gloves, his hands had been warm and reassuring.

This isn't what you came back here to do, Hannah.

She stood, taking another sip of her coffee. "Lecture's almost over, then. Drink your coffee, Dr. Mason."

"Greg." His head tilted to the side. "How many times do I have to ask?"

A hundred? A million?

That crazy hug all those months ago had changed something between them. Had left her with a frightening awareness of his scent, of the solid feel of his body against hers. She was only too eager to keep those memories locked up tight.

Calling him by his first name might just undo all that hard work, despite the fact that everyone else in the office called him Greg. Most of them would also admit to having a bit of a crush on their handsome employer. Or at least a good dose of hero-worship.

Some of his patients claimed he was a miracle worker.

In reality, Dr. Mason was just a man. He even had a pretty big flaw: despite his best efforts, he couldn't remain completely objective about his patients. And it ate him up from the inside out.

Mrs. Brookstone was a prime example of that.

He grieved. Deeply. For each one he lost. Even

though he didn't let others see his pain, she suspected he kept a private scorecard inside his head that recorded those he'd been able to snatch from death's door…and those he hadn't.

"Dr. Mason—"

His brows went up.

Okay, she was weak. Stupid. Would probably come to regret doing this very, very soon. But he was hurting right now.

"Greg," she corrected, her voice soft. "You can't save them all."

He dropped the pen onto the top of his desk, the sharp *ping* as it struck the wooden surface as loud as a guillotine strike. *Off with her head!*

Why had she said something he was already well aware of?

"Thank you."

His answer didn't track with what she'd just said. Unless he was being sarcastic.

But there was nothing in his face to indicate he was. In fact, his eyes met hers for a second or two before moving lower. Her lips tingled, sending an answering heat washing across her face.

He was *not* looking where she thought he was.

To cover up her embarrassment, she said, "What are you thanking me for?"

He picked up his prescription pad in one hand and his coffee cup in the other then stood. "For bringing me coffee." His lips curved up at the corners, sending more heat sloshing around her tummy. "And for saying my name."

CHAPTER TWO

THANK you for saying my name.

Greg rolled his eyes and scrubbed a hand across his head as he wrote up notes from his last patient of the day. What kind of lame comment was that?

He refused to admit he'd waited with bated breath, wondering if his physician's assistant would rise to the subtle challenge.

She had, which had shocked him. At first.

But hearing his name uttered in those husky tones had washed away his surprise and done a number on his gut. He'd been hounding her to adopt the informality of the rest of the staff for months now, but she'd steadfastly refused.

Until today.

And now he wondered if the policy he'd instituted hadn't been the most idiotic idea known to man.

She just felt sorry for you, that's all.

He slammed the folder shut, hoping to God she'd already left for the day. Unlike the first-name-basis rule, one of his smarter decisions had been to request that the staff leave once they'd finished inputting the last patient of the day, with the exception of his nurse. He might work long hours, but that didn't mean he should expect them to as well. Most of them had families to go home to.

Except Hannah.

He could still remember her gripping his neck, the softly whispered "Thank you" against his skin when her last set of test results had come back. And, like a fool, he'd returned her embrace... had—

Damn it. Why couldn't he get her out of his head today?

Maybe because she'd rarely given in once she'd made her mind up about something. Like not leaving his office this morning, until she'd watched him take a few sips of his coffee. He'd learned the hard way not to go head to head with her.

Her determination to make the most out of life had struck him even when he'd been her oncologist. It was still there now that he was her boss.

She hadn't been able to make the transition from patient to employee as well as some of his other staff had.

And yet that *"Greg"* had seemed to slip between

her lips effortlessly, as if she'd said it to herself hundreds of times before.

That thought made not only his collar tighten but other, more dangerous parts.

As her mouth had formed the word his thoughts had strayed, along with his eyes.

The pink color rushing to her face had told him she'd realized the exact second his gaze had touched her lips. Paused there.

He shook his head. What was wrong with him? He still had work to do and wanted to run by the hospital before it was too late to check on his patients.

Mrs. Brookstone's case had weighed on his heart like a rock all day. The last time he'd seen her, three of her grandchildren had crowded around her hospital bed, looking up at him with such hope. She'd had a pair of knitting needles balanced in her hands, in the process of making yet another hat for one of his patients.

But the news he'd brought had been anything but good.

Life was fragile. As he'd learned from experience. When Hannah had stood there in his office, all he'd wanted to do was pull her into his arms and relive the warmth of her breath washing across his cheek, the steady beat of her heart.

He'd resisted the impulse. Thank God.

Tucking a few files into his attaché case, he slung the strap over his shoulder and headed out, locking his office behind him. When he got to the closed door of the reception area, a strange blend of scents hit his nostrils. Garlic. Tomato sauce. It smelled like…lasagna.

What the…?

Someone must have brought pasta from home and heated it in the microwave at lunchtime.

His stomach gurgled in sad protest, and he realized he hadn't eaten anything other than the ham sandwich that had been mysteriously deposited on his desk at lunchtime.

Maybe he'd swing by the hospital cafeteria after making his rounds. He had nothing at home, other than the bacon and eggs he'd bought a couple of days ago. And neither of those sounded very appetizing right now. Especially with his nose still twitching in anticipation.

Pushing through the door, he blinked at the quartet of aluminum containers lining the reception desk. And the lights were still on.

"I was just about to come and get you." The voice

came from his left. He didn't have to look to know who it belonged to. Hannah.

He turned. Sure enough, there she was, her printed work smock gone and in its place a soft green blouse, cinched at the waist with a belt. The deep V-neckline drew his eyes down. He forced his gaze to stay above her collarbone, which was not quite as prominent as it had been during her treatments a year ago. That was a good sign. She was putting on some of the weight she'd lost. There were now curves that…

Clearing his throat, he met her gaze, noting the pink tinge from earlier was back in her cheeks. The color contrasted with her hair, the deep mahogany locks still fairly short, even after a year's regrowth. He liked the choppy style she'd adopted. It matched her personality. "I thought you'd left a while ago." He motioned toward the desk. "What's all this?"

"I figured you wouldn't stop to eat before going to the hospital, so I ordered takeout. Manicotti."

Huh. So his nose hadn't been too far off the mark. "I don't pay you to babysit me."

Her teeth came down on her lip, making him regret the words almost as soon as they'd left his mouth.

"I was trying to help. You work too hard."

One shoulder went up in irritation. "I think we've already covered this territory. I'm not married. No kids. So I don't think it's anyone's business how many hours I put in."

"Your patients count on you." Her voice was soft. Hesitant. And he had no idea what she meant. His patients were what motivated him to work so hard. Along with his sister's faith in him.

"I'm trying to make sure they have reason to."

She took a step closer. "No, I don't mean they need you to work harder. They count on you staying healthy enough to make good decisions."

Good decisions. A thread of anger unfurled inside his chest. He didn't need this today. Especially after Mrs. Brookstone. "I didn't hear you complaining when I treated you."

"No. But I didn't know what your office hours looked like back then." Her gaze went to the desk, and she picked her handbag up from a nearby chair and hitched it on her shoulder. "I didn't stay to argue with you. I just wanted to make sure you had a decent meal for once. I'll see you tomorrow."

"Wait." He put a hand on her arm, the shirt just as soft and silky as it appeared. He let go once she looked up at him. She'd said she was trying to help, and all he'd done was gripe and complain. "At least stay and eat with me. It'll be good to have a conversation that doesn't revolve around malignancies and treatment options."

She shook her head. "I don't think… There's only one plate."

"Then we'll improvise." Why was he insisting? Because her thoughtfulness had touched him? Because the perks of not having anyone waiting for him at home came with a hefty—and lonely—price tag?

He had no idea, but he knew he wanted some company. He didn't want to sit here by himself and dwell on his patients. What he'd said was true. There were times he craved conversation that had nothing to do with his job or his struggles—something his sister had intuitively known. But she wasn't here to make him smile anymore.

"Okay. Wait here."

The ease at which she'd given in surprised him almost as much as it had earlier. He smiled. He noticed she hadn't once said his name again, though.

She would before the meal was through. He'd see to it.

Punching the buzzer that unlocked the back area, she dragged a chair over to the door and propped it open, then disappeared for a few minutes. When she came back, she was holding a pink emesis basin.

"You're kidding."

She shrugged. "It's clean. I've eaten chili out one of these more than once."

Greg's lip curled half in disgust, half in amusement. "Have you ever thought of bringing in a package of paper plates and stashing them somewhere?"

"Yep, but I never got around to it. You said to improvise." Her head tilted, a quick smile forming. "This is me, improvising."

Okay, she had him there.

"And silverware? Are we supposed to share?" The thought made something heat in his chest.

She pulled a clear plastic package out from behind the desk. "Nope, the girls always keep their leftover plastic ware in case of an emergency."

What kind of emergency, other than eating, required sets of plastic knives and forks? He didn't think he wanted to know. "I guess we're all set, then."

Greg helped her dish out the food, noting she took the emesis basin for herself and gave him the plate and silverware provided by the restaurant. Besides the manicotti, there were two kinds of sauce, white and red, as well as a Caesar salad and garlic rolls. She'd expected him to eat all this himself?

"I see I owe you some money."

She shook her head, spooning white sauce over her own portion. "I took money out of the petty-cash drawer."

His brows went up. "We keep that much in there?"

"Fifty bucks." She dropped the spoon back into the container. "But this pretty much cleaned it out."

He couldn't remember the last time he'd spent that much money on a meal for himself. The warmth in his chest grew, bringing with it the uncomfortable awareness that he was in a deserted medical building with a woman he couldn't begin to understand. One he found dangerously attractive.

She was also one of his employees. Asking her to stay and eat with him had been a big mistake. Huge!

But he couldn't very well ask her to leave now.

So he sat on one of the brown leatherette chairs in the waiting room next to her, balancing a flimsy plate across his knees.

Hannah, on the other hand, looked perfectly at home, cutting into her manicotti with a plastic fork and popping a piece into her mouth. "Mmm." Her lids came down for a brief second as she seemed to savor the food.

He swallowed, despite the fact that he had nothing in his mouth other than the lump that was currently stuck in his throat.

Incredibly long lashes swept back up, and green eyes regarded him. "Aren't you going to taste it?"

The only thing he wanted to taste were her lips. *Ah, hell.*

He forked up a big bite and shoved it past his teeth, dumping the food onto his tongue before he could do or say anything stupid. He chewed. Swallowed. His stomach gave another fierce rumble.

Okay, so she'd been right. He was hungry. And evidently that fact was going to trump any other urges for the moment. He relaxed into his seat, figuring he could eat and then get the hell out of there before his belly figured out it was full and let his other instincts out of their cage. "It's good."

"I know. It's my go-to place for takeout. I order from there at least once a week."

He didn't like to think of Hannah at home alone, eating from disposable metal containers. But it wasn't much better than what he did day in and day out. He was content with it, so why would he assume someone else wouldn't be?

Greg just couldn't imagine her having weekends free, figuring she'd be out making up for the year she'd lost. There was something inside her that burned brightly. That glow could have been snuffed out in an instant. Not something he wanted to think about right now.

He covered by saying, "I normally just grab something from the hospital cafeteria."

"I know."

She did?

Before he could ask, she added, "I used to see you walking down the corridor with a sandwich container in your hand."

"When...?"

"When I was getting my chemo infusions. I saw you sometimes." Her hand went to her collarbone area and fingered the pale scar where her port had once been. Greg was so used to seeing those that he hadn't even noticed it.

He also hadn't realized she'd been in that treatment room. Had seen him. How many other patients had he walked by without noticing? Another brick of guilt settled into place. "I'm sorry. I'm normally so busy, I don't stop in there all the time."

Putting her fork into her bowl, she reached out and touched his hand. "I wasn't trying to make you feel bad. I've just learned how important it is to eat a balanced meal."

She was right. Again. He often preached to his patients that they needed to strengthen their bodies as much as possible to help during the chemo treatments as well as to aid in the fight of their disease. That meant making healthy choices when it came to food. And yet, just like a pulmonologist who indulged in the occasional cigarette, Greg was unwilling to abide by his own advice.

"I don't have cancer, but I also don't cook."

She picked up her fork again, avoiding his eyes this time. "That's why there are places like *Piazza Toscana*." The comment, unlike her lighthearted ones from a few moments ago, was tight, as if…

I don't have cancer.

How damned insensitive could he be? She'd spent a year undergoing chemotherapy. Hadn't known for sure if she'd live or die.

Maybe she was right. He worked so hard that he no longer paid attention to social conventions or cared how his words might affect someone else.

No, that wasn't right. He did care.

Setting his plate onto the chair next to him, he shifted sideways to face her. "Hey." He waited until she looked at him before continuing. "I'm sorry for saying that. There's no good reason, other than I'm tired and not thinking straight."

She blinked, and he wasn't sure whether the light was playing tricks on him or if there'd been a trace of moisture rimming her lower lids. But when he looked closer, it was gone.

"How long will you be at the hospital tonight?" she asked.

"About an hour."

Glancing at her watch, she set her own plate to the side and went over to the low sofa and picked up one of the leather pillows. Coming back, she lowered herself to the padded loop carpet at his feet.

His mouth went dry as she set the pillow down and patted the area next to her. "It's only seven. Why don't you stretch out for a while? Take a quick nap. I promise I won't let you sleep longer than an hour."

Was she crazy? After the thoughts that had just gone spinning through his head? There was no way he was going to lie down on the floor and—

Even as the words slid through his mind, a wave of exhaustion washed over him, staggering him with its force.

It was the food. The heavy meal was making him sleepy.

What would it hurt? If his eyes were shut, he could block out her face. No more trying to make small talk. No more worrying about how he was looking at her. About what her kneeling on the floor with that pillow had made him imagine.

Before he was fully aware of what he was doing, he'd done as she'd suggested and stretched out on his back, his head on the pillow she'd laid next to her hip. Every muscle in his body seemed to go boneless, and he glanced up to see her leaning over him with a smile. Her fingers brushed across his forehead, the touch light. Comforting.

He pulled in a deep breath. Let it out.

"Close your eyes, Greg. I promise I'll be right here."

Even as his lids seemed to obey her every command, a tired sense of triumph went through him.

He'd been right. She'd said his name. Again.

CHAPTER THREE

THE trill of Hannah's watch alarm registered in her ears, but it took her brain a little more time to place the sound.

Opening her eyes, she punched a button before noticing Greg's dark, mussed hair, his even darker eyes regarding her with a slight smile. He was upside down. No, wait. She was. Hadn't she been sitting up while he'd slept? Why were they now reversed?

Ack. Because she'd fallen asleep, too. Had evidently just keeled over sideways and was lying on the floor, looking pretty much like she'd looked sitting up. Bent at the hips, legs straight out.

Greg's lips curved higher. "Looks like I wasn't the only one who was tired."

Only he didn't seem tired. Not anymore. His eyes glittered with life, and the dark circles beneath them had eased. He also looked much more relaxed. Or was that still due to the topsy-turvy world she'd awoken into? Maybe his smile was really a frown.

"Did you sleep well?" She cleared her throat when her voice came out as a hoarse squawk.

"Like a rock. Good thing you set that alarm."

He could say that again. She'd only set it so she wouldn't be tempted to wake him with the proverbial kiss. Like a reverse Sleeping Beauty. That analogy fit her current mixed-up thought processes to a T. "Sorry. I had no idea I was that tired."

"I should be the one saying sorry. I don't expect you to keep the same hours I do."

Her eyes narrowed slightly, and somewhere in the back of her mind, she realized she should be moving. "Don't you think I'm capable of it?"

He gave a soft laugh. "Oh, I know you are. I just don't want you to run you off before I've…"

His words trailed away.

"Before you've what?"

"Before I've proven I can take better care of myself."

That made her smile. But when she did try to sit up, the awkward angle at which she'd been lying made her back muscles give a warning twinge. She eased back down, licking her lips as she waited for the spasm to pass.

He frowned. "What is it?"

"Nothing." Lord, what was she going to do? She couldn't very well wave him off and send him on his way while pretzeled on the floor. What if she couldn't get up after he left and he returned in the morning to find her still here? Still folded like a crazed contortionist? "I'll be fine in a minute. My...er, foot's asleep."

He angled away, his gaze sweeping down her pants' legs. He reached down and plucked off one of her white leather slip-ons and then the other. "Which one?"

"No, don't touch it!"

Okay, that screech hadn't been exactly the calm tone she'd been going for. But her feet were seriously ticklish—one wrong move and she'd wrench her back even further.

"Shh. I won't." He propped himself on one elbow as he continued to regard her. "Your foot might keep you from walking but it wouldn't keep you from sitting up. Why didn't you at least get a pillow for yourself?"

Because I didn't expect to crash to the floor like a felled tree. Was so busy watching each breath you took that...

No, that wasn't right. She'd been merely biding her time, letting him get some much-needed rest.

"I just closed my eyes for a second or two."

"Or more." He paused, still watching her face. "Do you want me to help you up?"

Her body tensed, her back already sending up a frantic mayday. "No." She even managed to smile, although she could only imagine what it looked like to him. She'd better come clean before he did something that made the situation worse. "My back is a little...sore. From lying in this position."

"I thought it was your foot?"

"I lied." The admission came with a real smile this time.

"Hannah, Hannah, what am I going to do with you?" The soft murmur trailed across her senses, making her back tighten further.

She pulled in a careful breath. "How about leaving me to die in peace?"

His face stilled. "Don't say that."

"Don't say...?" It hit her. Mrs. Brookstone's turn for the worse. How hard he'd worked to keep that from happening to any of his patients. "Sorry."

"It's okay." He stood up and carefully lifted the chair behind her out of the way. Then the two on either side of it.

"What are you doing?"

"I'm going to help you sit up."

"I don't think that's a good idea."

When he knelt on the floor behind her and put his hands on the muscles on her right side, a quick flicker of fear went through her. But he didn't try to jerk her upright. Instead his fingers played over the different areas of her back before muttering something under his breath. Then he said, "I can't feel anything through your shirt. I need bare skin."

Her heart went into overdrive, threatening to hammer its way out of her chest. "Wh-what?"

"Sorry. I meant your muscles." He paused. "Where does it hurt?"

"Below my right shoulderblade."

His fingers shifted, testing. "Can you roll onto your stomach?"

"I don't know." She tried, inching to the right, his palms taking some of the work off her back muscles. Then she was there, legs stretched straight behind her, feet bare, all the while a group of muscles sizzled with fire. Even drawing too deep a breath caused it to tighten further. A tiny whimper made its way out before she could stop it.

His fingers began exploring her back again until

he reached the ball of agony around which her world currently swirled.

"Oh, God, don't. Please." She was horrified at the hoarse plea in her voice.

He swore softly.

"Stay here. I'm going to get a muscle relaxant and a heating pad. I'll be right back."

As he walked away, Hannah heard him talking softly to someone, giving them his cell number and asking whoever it was to call him if there was an emergency. The hospital? His answering service?

She hadn't wanted to interfere with his work. She'd just wanted to leave some food for him and be on her way.

He could have just left her, like she'd suggested…

But he wasn't that kind of man.

She heard him come back. "I don't want you to take the pill lying down like that, so we'll see if we can loosen you up a little first."

Despite the pain, she giggled. It sounded more like he was trying to get her drunk than help her get back on her feet.

"You find this funny?"

"No. It's just… Never mind."

A second later he draped something across the sore part of her back and the sound of a switch clicking hit her ears. Soft vibrations made their way through her back, not hard enough to hurt but enough that she knew it was there.

"It'll warm up in a minute or two."

"I'm sorry. I don't normally have back spasms." The last time had been after her biopsy, when lying in one position for a prolonged period of time had left her muscles stiff and sore. She'd moved too quickly and driven home in quiet agony, too embarrassed to tell anyone at the hospital what was going on. It had taken two days for the pain to ease—she hadn't even been able to lift her arm to brush her hair. And it had been in the same muscle group as now.

What if she were laid up for two days again? No. If she could just get up, she'd be fine.

Greg's voice came back to her. "It's okay. Just rest a few more minutes."

Unable to do anything else, she watched as he cleaned up the remainder of their shared meal, tossing containers into one of the trash cans and drawing the plastic bag up tight.

Sure enough, the vibrating pad began to warm, the heat working its way into the affected muscle. It didn't completely relax but the pain wasn't quite as severe as it had been moments earlier. Maybe she could… Shifting a bit, she gasped as the muscle contracted again.

"Lie still. You're not going anywhere for a couple of hours."

A couple of hours? A second ago he'd said to rest for a few minutes.

"Why don't you go to the hospital and then head home? I'll be fine in a little while. Promise."

"Not going to happen, Hannah. The hospital can do without me for one night. I've already told them to call me if there's an emergency."

Guilt rolled through her. He never skipped his rounds that she knew of. Always did them every night. Even weekends.

And here he was, stuck at the office, babysitting the person who'd told him to get some rest. Having to take care of her. Again. Just like during her treatments.

The thought brought tears to her eyes. She never wanted to go back to those days of fear and pain and that dark hole that had threatened to close over the top of her.

Stop it. You're not sick. It's just a muscle cramp.

The pain would soon be gone then she'd be strong and healthy once again. Free to live every day to the fullest. She visualized those words, made them her reality. Added an image of herself with a rounded tummy and pink, glowing cheeks. She was happy. Content.

Pregnant.

She blinked, remembering the procedure she'd undergone just that morning. She also realized her back was feeling better, at least while she was lying still. If she could just stay where she was a few minutes longer…

A half hour later, she found herself again nodding off, the pain finally sliding away. The vibrations stopped and she was aware of the heating pad being lifted off and gentle hands again moving over her back, this time right where it had hurt. She pulled in a deep breath and felt nothing but that contentment she'd reached for a few minutes earlier. "It's gone." She whispered the words, afraid the pain would find her again if she spoke any louder.

"I'm sorry. Do you want me to put it back?"

"Put it…?" She realized he was talking about the heating pad. "No, I meant my back feels better. Can you help me sit up?"

"Yes, but we're going to roll you onto your back first so you won't have to twist at an awkward angle. I don't want to give that muscle any reason to flare up again." He placed his hands on her right shoulder and hip. "Ready?"

His fingers were almost as warm as the heating pad and a tiny shudder went through her. "I'm ready."

"On three." He counted slowly and when he reached three, before she could even brace her hands on the floor and help, he'd gently rolled her over.

Moving a tiny bit, she tested her muscles. Nothing felt out of place or sore.

His brown eyes slid over her face. "Everything okay?"

"I think so."

"Let's just wait a minute or two." He nodded toward the reception desk. "I have some carisoprodol, just in case."

She shifted again, a little more this time, to see if anything acted up. Still nothing. "I think the worst is over. And I'd rather not drive with that kind of medication in my system."

"I'll take you home."

"Muscle relaxants knock me for a loop, and I'm never myself the next day." She didn't want to tell him that her year of treatment had conditioned her throat to constrict at the sight of anything that resembled a capsule. "I have to work tomorrow, remember?"

"Stay home."

She lifted her hand, feeling at a distinct disadvantage lying flat on her back. "Help me up, and then we'll talk about it."

Greg stood and then curled his hand around hers. She sensed a slight hesitation on his part before his grip tightened and his arm bent at the elbow as he applied steady pressure. Their connected palms were doing crazy things to her stomach so, in an effort to hurry the process up, she braced her feet and launched herself into a vertical position.

Her momentum carried her straight into his chest where she landed with a thump.

Ack!

Greg wrapped an arm around her waist, holding her against his solid body as she tried to catch her breath.

At least her stupid move hadn't sent her back into another spasm.

Something she couldn't say about her heart, which was pumping at an alarming rate. A hundred and twenty beats per minute at least…and rising by the second.

She tried to act nonchalant, as if falling against

her employer was something she did on a regular basis. And it was no big deal. She'd hugged him before after all. "Sorry. I guess I shouldn't have gotten up so fast."

"I'll say." The murmured words ruffled her hair and sent her heart on another race for the finish line. "How's your back?"

She wiggled the upper part of her body back and forth to feel it out, then realized she'd just done a quick shimmy against his thorax.

Her nipples contracted in reaction, and she blurted out the first thing she could think of: "Can't feel a thing."

The hand at her back tightened. "Can't you?"

Um, yeah. And it wasn't good. Because she was suddenly aware of every inch of male flesh pressed against her. Muscular chest, firm abs, taut thighs, and…

No, it couldn't be. She licked her lips, telling herself to pull back now before he realized that *she* realized that he was…

He was…

Yes. He *was*.

And if she shifted one millimeter, she'd be rubbing right against his *was*. Lord, did she want to press just a little bit.

And like that horrible thing that often happened when you told yourself not to do something—like not to eat that whole pint of ice cream in one sitting—your body did the exact opposite.

She pressed.

And the sound of his breath hissing in through his teeth met her ears.

Okay. Now he knew that she knew.

She slowly lifted her head and met eyes that were sizzling with something she hadn't seen in a very long time in a man. Especially not directed at her.

Desire.

Steaming. Naked. Toe-curling need.

"Greg?" She had no idea why she said his name, but his gaze darkened further.

One hand came up and slid into her hair, his thumb resting along her jaw. "How's your back?"

"Better." The words came out in a whisper, because suddenly she knew why he was asking. She emphasized her point. "*Much* better."

"Hannah." His thumb applied gentle pressure to tilt her head up, even as he angled his own down until only a breath of space remained between them. "You know this is a very bad idea."

"Worse than playing with matches?"

"Much worse."

It was. But the fascination of running that match across a strike plate and watching it flare to life proved too much to resist. Besides, she wasn't sure she even had what it took to light that particular fire. Closing her eyes, she bridged the gap between them, deciding to prove him right…and herself wrong.

He didn't want her. Couldn't.

The second her lips met his, though, and the hand at her nape hauled her even closer, she knew.

He could.

And he did.

CHAPTER FOUR

GREG wasn't sure who kissed whom first, but he knew with certainty there was nowhere he'd rather be right now. First she'd coaxed him to eat. Then to sleep. When he'd awoken, he'd found her right there beside him—even if she had been folded into something reminiscent of a cube. Her mouth had been slightly open, one hand curled softly against her chest. Her breasts had slowly risen and fallen as she'd breathed. The sight had sent his endocrine system on a rampage, pumping chemicals through his body. Then she'd looked up with those big green eyes, and he'd been lost. He'd stayed where he was, when he should have run.

No, that wasn't completely true. He'd been pretty sure he could walk away without a problem, until that singular moment when her hips had seemed to zero in on a certain part of his anatomy. The part that was now issuing all sorts of commands he wasn't sure he could resist.

He tilted his head, deepening the kiss, ready to pull back at the first sign of hesitation on her part.

Damn it, what was he thinking? Her back had just gone through hell and back, and here he was, mauling her to within an inch of her life.

But wasn't she mauling him right back, her fists buried in his starched shirt and hanging on for dear life?

Still, he had to be sure.

"Your back," he whispered against her lips.

"Forgotten."

"But—"

She pulled him close and cut off his words with another lingering kiss.

Okay, if that's the way she wanted to play this, who was he to complain? Besides, he was tired of warring against his emotions, trying to keep them in check so as not to alarm his patients, or hand out undue hope, if things took a turn for the worse.

Like with Martha Brookstone?

No, don't think of that right now.

He was with someone who'd fought the disease. Who'd won. He gloried in that. Celebrated Hannah's life. Her health. It was why he'd surrounded himself with people just like her, to remind himself that cancer could be beaten. Not all of the time. His own sister had…

His fingers tightened in Hannah's hair, desperate to feel the life force coursing through her body, her heart pumping strongly against his own.

Life! This was what it was about. The need for closeness, to reaffirm your own existence.

Surely just this once he could block out the real world.

The blinds were closed. Door locked. Alarm set.

And, most of all, there was a beautiful, willing woman in his arms.

Her low sigh melted his resistance even further, and Greg gentled his kiss, taking the time to taste her, to measure the softness of her lips against his. His tongue slid in a slow arc across the surface of her teeth, then back again, his senses roaring to life when she opened her mouth in invitation. Stunned by the force of his reaction, he hung around outside for a second or two, until her tongue touched the underside of his, leading him inside. Coaxing him, just like she'd done with his meal. Before he knew it, he was right there, the interplay of textures and heat making it impossible for him to retreat again.

His hand left her hair, sliding down her back

until it lay just above the curve of her buttocks. A very dangerous place to be. Once he took that leap there'd be no going back.

On that note, he lingered in her mouth, needing to show her exactly what she was doing to him, and that if she intended to call a halt to things, it needed to be soon.

She didn't. She met each stroke by moving closer, protested each withdrawal with a soft bite to his lower lip. His hands slid down and over in unison, his fingers curving on the rounded flesh he found there. It filled his palms, set his whole body on fire.

He pulled her up and against him, hoping to relieve a little of the ache that was growing steadily worse. And hoping the shock would knock them both back into the realm of reality. Except Greg didn't want reality. He wanted the fantasy...to keep her here. With him. Wanted to wish their clothing gone and to drive every last inch of himself into her—to fill her to capacity and beyond.

Hannah released her hold on his shirt, and at first he thought she meant to pull away. Instead, the top button of his shirt popped free, as if...

His lips left hers in question, and he caught her smile. Then another button was plucked loose.

She was undoing his shirt. There went the third button. It was either allow her to keep going or let go of her and stop her.

Her hands settled on his bare chest, upping the ante. Especially when they wandered down, purposely sliding over his nipples in the process. His eyes squeezed shut as he tried to hold on to some small portion of his sanity.

When her fingers seemed to want to stay and visit for a while, teasing and testing, he had no choice. He let go of her, reaching up to capture her wrists and carry them behind her back.

"You're treading on dangerous ground."

Her brows went up. "I hadn't even gotten to the dangerous part yet."

Greg couldn't stop a quick laugh of surprise. This was a side of Hannah he hadn't known existed. But he liked it.

He took her mouth again. Harder this time. His free hand slid beneath her blouse and claimed the very thing he'd just denied her, the lacy bra providing almost no barrier. And he reveled in it—in the tightly drawn nipple that pressed against the fabric and scraped lusciously against his palm. When he rolled the bud between his thumb and forefinger, she moaned into his mouth.

Yes.

God, he wanted her. Now.

He let go of her and grasped the bottom of her blouse, holding her gaze as she slowly raised her arms above her head so he could take it off. Her shirt was as far as he got, though, because she reached back and unhooked the black bra herself, letting it fall from her body. Still no sign that her back was bothering her. But, hell, if the sight of her naked breasts didn't hurt him in a very different kind of way.

When he started to move forward again, she backed up a step and reached for the button of her slacks. "Here's where it starts getting dangerous."

Holy hell. Surely she didn't mean to…

In an instant she'd unzipped them and pushed them down her hips, kicking them away from her. Her black panties were barely there, just a scrap of lace with a crisscrossing of strings on the sides. He had no idea where they led or what the back looked like, and he wasn't sure he wanted to know.

"Hannah," he warned, when her fingertips slipped beneath the ties.

She gave a soft laugh. "Your turn, then."

His turn to what? Take off his clothes? Remove her last article of clothing himself?

He assumed she meant for him to start shucking his own clothes, so he finished unbuttoning his shirt and slung the garment to the side. His fingers weren't quite as steady as hers, but it had been a long time since he'd been with anyone. A very long time. His hours were too crazy, and he was too exhausted by the time he got home.

And yet right now he seemed to have the energy of an eighteen-year-old boy.

Hannah moved back in before he could go any further and slid her palms up his chest, and rested them on his shoulders, leaning in to kiss the base of his throat.

That wasn't where he wanted her. "Hey."

When she looked up, he took her mouth, wrapping his arms around the bare skin of her back, trying to absorb everything at once. The heat of her skin against his, the softness of her breasts.

Breasts he wanted to devour.

He gripped her hips, intending to ease her back so he could cup them, but the strings on her panties sidetracked him. He followed them around. The back had a satiny feel as opposed to the lace in front. Part of him was relieved, part of him disappointed. He'd half hoped to find nothing there.

But it didn't matter, because he could just do this…

He slid his fingers between the elastic band and her skin and repeated on her bare bottom what he'd done earlier when she'd still been wearing pants. He squeezed, trying to get his fill, then pulled back enough to push her underwear halfway down her legs, his mouth having to leave hers to do so. This time when his hands returned to their perch, he pulled her tight against him, her bare flesh pressing directly on the hard bulge at the front of his slacks. He ground against her, once…twice, swallowing hard when she gave a tiny whimper, her fingers digging into his shoulders.

Enough!

He scooped her up in his arms in a quick movement and carried her past the still-propped-open doorway in back. His office had a couch.

And a desk.

Yes.

That's where he wanted her. On his desk, legs splayed open, with him between them. His flesh tightened beyond belief.

That decadent image would carry him through many a lonely night.

And there'd be no danger of hurting her back.

He gave a rough laugh.

Sure. That was the reason.

He pushed on the handle, but it didn't budge. Damn. Locked.

"Where's the key?" she whispered.

"Left front pocket." Thank heavens he'd kept his trousers on.

"I think I can get it." Hannah scooched her arm between their bodies, her breasts jiggling in a way that made his mouth water. She found his pocket, dipped in and instead of finding his keys and retreating, her hand drifted to the right and curved over the tight ridge of flesh. The fingers massaged and squeezed and drove the breath from his lungs.

"Those aren't my keys, woman."

She gave a soft laugh. "I know." Her nails scraped down his length, the fabric keeping it from hurting while also making it the most erotic sensation he'd ever felt. He almost did the unthinkable standing right there in front of his door.

"Hannah…please."

She kissed the side of his neck and retrieved his keys. "I like it when you say please."

That "please" now encompassed asking God to help him make it inside his office.

"Unlock the door."

He turned his body sideways to allow her to reach the lock, which she undid in record time. Pushing his way past the door, he carried her over to his desk. He surveyed it, trying to figure out where to put her. "Push the pencil cup onto the floor."

Her brows went up, but she did as he asked, the offending object flying off the side of the desk, shedding pens and pencils as it went. He then set her on the edge and stepped back to watch her as he undid his own pants.

He was afraid she'd get up, but she didn't. She sat there, panties still halfway down her legs, her arms going back to prop herself on the wide wooden surface. The act pushed her breasts up and out, while pushing his self-control to the breaking point.

Making short work of the rest of his clothes, he moved over to her and rested his arms on either side of her hips. He gave her a long, slow smile. "My turn to get a little dangerous."

"Believe me, you already are."

Her tongue came out to moisten her lips. He leaned in and did the same, drawing his tongue slowly across her already wet mouth. He then kissed her chin, before nudging her head back so he had access to the underside of her throat. Working his way down to her shoulder, he dipped further until he reached her right breast.

The second his lips closed over her nipple, he knew it had been worth the wait. Her reaction was immediate. She arched toward him with a moan. But when she went to lift her arms, he put his hands over hers, trapping them on the desk.

She thought she could drive him crazy with no recourse? Well, he was about to get a little of his own back. He suckled and nibbled, holding her in place with his teeth while his tongue lapped over her. When he finally released her, the nipple was slick and tight.

Just like she would be when he finally entered her. And it had to be soon.

He finally stood upright. Hannah's teeth were digging into her lower lip, eyes sealed shut. Her hips made tiny movements on the surface of his desk.

He wanted to be right in the middle of that.

He slid her panties the rest of the way down her legs, and as soon as they were gone, her thighs spread apart. He swallowed as he moved between them, trying to think about anything other than what was about to happen, and failing miserably. Instead, he gave her a deep open-mouthed kiss, settling against her and finding her just as slick and ready as he'd hoped.

To be sure, he slid his hand between them, thumb seeking the right spot and then stroking gently. She pressed closer, moaning against his mouth. Her flesh enveloped his tip, the heat and tightness driving him to the very edge of insanity. It was all he could do not to thrust into her and lose himself in a fiery rush. As if reading his thoughts, she reached around to grab his butt, pulling him even deeper.

She was so wet, so hot. Her hips were still making those tiny thrusting motions against his arousal...against his thumb. Growing stronger. Quicker.

He sped up the motion of his thumb, knowing that the second she went over the edge, he was going with her. And he'd be able to push deeper. Harder.

No! Wait. Condom!

He started to withdraw, only to have her hands pull at him desperately, her calves wrapping around him, hips sliding forward until she had him fully within her. She lay back on the desk, her eyes pleading with him.

"Greg, now. Please."

The sight of her lying naked on top of his desk

drove every rational thought he'd had a few seconds ago from his mind. Grasping her hips, he pushed into her, reveling in the tight heat that gripped him to perfection. She put her heels on the edge of the desk and rose to meet him stroke for stroke, beads of sweat breaking out on his forehead as he fought for control.

Control he couldn't seem to find.

No need because Hannah was at the end of hers as well, pushing herself onto him, her hips now leaving the desk every time he drove into her. Within a few seconds she arched up and gasped, her body tightening around him in a series of explosive waves. He gave up and held on for dear life, hands braced on the desk as he thrust into her again and again, her name falling from his lips as he found his own release deep inside her.

He went down onto his elbows as the world slowed, as time began to trickle back to normal. Hannah's breath floated past his cheek, her sweet, womanly scent washing over him as he struggled to piece together what had just happened.

No need to ask. He already knew.

Hannah had happened. And he realized he'd been trying to avoid this moment for months. Definitely since that fateful hug. Maybe even the entire time he'd known her.

And as reality crystallized, hardening into a rock that blocked his throat—filled his chest—another realization swept over him. This one much more deadly.

His wallet contained an object around which his thoughts and regrets now circled like vultures.

A single, unopened condom.

CHAPTER FIVE

HORRIFIED.

The word she'd been searching for all morning finally came to mind. The one adjective that described Greg's face when he'd caught his breath enough to stand upright and look down at her. Not regret. Not joy. Not satisfied exhaustion.

Horror.

It was an expression she'd never forget.

Her cheeks burned as she balled up the used exam-table paper and tossed it in the waste receptacle to prepare the room for the next patient. How was she going to get up the nerve to walk into his office and look at that desk? The second she did, would her mind picture him going down on his elbows in those final few seconds, would she remember her own soft cries of pleasure filling the room?

Oh, God.

The man had helped her up afterward, and they'd dressed without a word. Had collected their things, walked through the office and out the front door in silence. Until she'd inserted the key into her car door, only to have a hand cover hers, stopping her from fleeing into the night.

"Hannah, I'm sorry. We'll talk…later."

Sorry. The very word she'd dreaded hearing. It ranked right up there with *horrified* and *talk.*

She didn't want to talk. Or even face him.

He was in surgery this morning, leaving Hannah with a full slate of patients who needed her to be on her game. And no time to plan what she'd say when she eventually saw him again.

And she would.

Unless she quit. The idea had come to her the night before, tickling her with temptation before she dismissed it as ridiculous. She needed this job, especially now. What had happened last night was a fluke. Greg had been hurting, and she'd botched her attempt to comfort him by sending out the wrong signals.

No. That was a lie. They had been the right signals, and he'd picked up on them as easily as the PET scan had homed in on the cancer in her lymph nodes.

Stella poked her head into the room. "Are you ready for the next patient?"

"Yep." She forced a smile, knowing it probably looked as strained as she felt.

"You okay?" The receptionist's concern only made her feel worse, because she was far from all right.

Why couldn't her little encounter with Greg have happened two weeks from now? A month? Anything outside the five-day lifespan of sperm? And with the washed sperm used during inseminations, that window was even narrower.

If she got pregnant now, nothing other than a D.N.A. test could prove whether the baby was the donor's or Greg's.

"Hannah?" Stella's voice broke through her thoughts.

"Sorry. I'm fine. Just daydreaming."

Or nightmaring, whichever you chose to call it.

The receptionist stepped inside the room and closed the door. "About anyone I know?"

"No." The word came out on a strange wobbly note, and she decided some kind of explanation was due. "I had an I.U.I. procedure yesterday, and I was thinking about the possibilities."

And that was the absolute truth.

"Oh, honey, congratulations!" Stella enveloped her in a bear hug, and if the fifty-year-old's ebullience was in direct proportion to the tightness of the squeeze, it was off the charts, since she'd just wrung the last molecule of air from Hannah's lungs.

Her brain a bit woozy from the lack of oxygen, she hurried to add, "I don't even know if it took yet or not, so please don't tell anyone."

Especially not their boss.

All she needed was for Greg to hear she was pregnant the second he walked into the office.

He'd immediately wonder if she was angling for something, since there's no way she could know twelve hours out whether or not he'd knocked her up.

Right.

Horrified would be the least of her worries, if that happened. And *looking for a new job* would be the order of the day.

"Don't worry. My lips are sealed."

Since those lips tended to flap around like pancakes tossed from a cast-iron skillet, this could mean trouble. Which meant she'd have to talk to Greg, like it or not.

Too bad she couldn't rewind to yesterday and go back to calling him Dr. Mason. Only if she did that now, he'd assume she was doing it because of their little interlude, and he'd be right. No, the less emphasis she placed on what had happened, the less likely it was to change their working relationship.

"Okay, Stella, where's our next patient?"

The next two hours passed in a frenzy of work and worry. She forced the latter to remain in the background, only letting it surface when she had five minutes to spare, which was thankfully not often.

Her last patient of the day sat on the exam table, a jewel-toned silk scarf artfully draped around her head. The woman's blue eyes sparkled with life. Claire Taylor had already defied the odds once and was well on her way to doing it a second time. The lumpectomy she'd had three years ago was now a mastectomy scar, but she was cheerful and positive. Since her first diagnosis, the twenty-six-year-old had gotten married and was already looking ahead to a bright future.

"I talked to a plastic surgeon last week about reconstruction."

Hannah glanced up from her examination. "I didn't realize you were even thinking about it." Claire had opted not to have the reconstruction right after the surgery. She'd been through a chemo regimen once before and didn't want to have to worry about anything but getting through that ordeal. She was halfway through her eight-treatment cycle—heading down the home stretch.

"I wasn't. But I haven't been as sick this time as I was the last time. Or maybe I just remember it being worse because I didn't know what to expect."

Hannah could relate to that. She'd saved her scarves—all fifty of them—as a reminder that she was a survivor, and that she intended to keep on living. Every once in a while she wore one around her neck and talked about it with her patients. As one survivor to another.

Maybe Claire was at that point as well—gearing up to tell the world she was ready to enjoy the rest of her life. "What did the surgeon say?"

"That he could take some skin from my stomach to construct the breast. So I'd get a tummy tuck and a perky new boob at the same time."

"Wow, a twofer—you lucky girl."

Right as she said it, she winced, realizing she'd also gotten one of those: two batches of sperm for the price of one. But in this case she could have done without the figurative tummy tuck and been perfectly happy sticking to the lab-generated portion.

Claire laughed. "I know, right?"

"What does your husband think of all this?"

"Oh, you know how they are. He claims to love me just as I am, says I don't need it." The woman's lips twisted. "So who said I was doing it for him, anyway?"

It was Hannah's turn to laugh. "Did you tell him that?'

"No way. Let him think it. It'll add some spice to our love life."

Hannah could feel the heat crawling up her stomach on its way to her face. The sound of a knock and then the door opening didn't help, especially when Greg strolled in, his face a study in exhaustion. But when he saw Claire, his eyes softened, the edges of his mouth turning up in a smile. "I couldn't let one of my favorite patients get away without a single hello."

Claire laughed. "Okay, then. Hello."

Had he really come back to the office to say hi his patients? Or was he here to have the Dreaded Talk?

Why hadn't he just gone home? This could wait. She was tired too, and she wasn't up to a conversation about regrets.

He continued talking to his patient, not giving

Hannah a second glance as he listened intently to Claire's plans for surgery. He held out a hand for the chart, which Hannah gave him. A moment passed as he perused the contents, flipping pages. "I'd like it if you waited until after you complete the regimen, just to be sure. You'll be stronger and there'll be less worry about infection."

"That's what the surgeon said, as well." Her hand crept up to the robe, and the hollow left by the mastectomy. "It's healing well, and he says I'm a good candidate."

"I agree. There's no reason to think you wouldn't be. Let's just get you through the next couple of months."

Maybe that's what she needed to focus on: getting through the next couple of months. Well… nine, in her case.

Standing in the hallway with Greg while Claire got dressed, she cast about for something to say that would send him on his way. But he didn't seem in a hurry to leave, leaning against the wall, watching her.

Why was he doing that? Why hadn't he just gone straight to his office and let her finish up with the patient?

"How did surgery go?"

"Pretty well."

"This was the Hodgkin's patient, right?" She tried to get him to keep talking, in part to prevent the silence from growing more awkward but also because this was a diagnosis close to her heart.

At his nod, she pressed forward. "Did you have to perform a splenectomy?"

"She was in the early stages, so yes." He paused and glanced down the hallway toward his office. "I don't like doing them, but..."

"I know." Her fingers itched to go to his arm and reassure him, but she didn't dare. "I'm doing fine without mine, though."

"Sometimes it's the only way to know for sure how much lymph-node involvement there is."

Hodgkin's cells tended to collect in the spleen early in the disease. Hers had been removed for the same reason.

Before she could reply, Claire came through the door, her huge handbag slung over her shoulder. "Thanks, guys. I appreciate it."

"I'll try to peek in on you at the hospital during your next treatment. When do you go in?"

Hannah's brows went up. Since when did he do that? He'd never come into the chemo room when she'd been having her infusions. And it wasn't like his time wasn't sucked in every direction under the sun already. They saw Claire off and then she turned to face him. "Are you doing that for all your patients now?"

"Doing what?"

"Checking in on them during chemo treatments."

He pulled his shoulder off the wall and stood straighter. "When I'm at the hospital, I try to."

A small ache went through her heart. "You're going to kill yourself, you know." She wasn't sure whether or not she should follow that thought, but the words just kind of came out. "I know what it's like to wonder if you have a tomorrow. It's made me grab at life and enjoy every second I have."

His eyes met hers, and his jaw tightened. "Some of us don't have that option."

"That's ridiculous. You have as much choice as the next person."

A hard laugh echoed through the hallway. "I see. And your way of enjoying life is to do whatever strikes your fancy at that particular moment—especially after business hours—no matter what the consequences?"

The inference was plain.

She glanced down the hall, hoping no one was within earshot. "Maybe that's what's needed sometimes. Less thinking, more doing." Hannah didn't believe that for a second, but she wasn't about to admit how much his attitude hurt. There was almost an accusatory slant to his tone that made her wonder if he really felt that way about her.

He stared at her for several seconds then sighed. "I think we need to have that talk before this goes any further."

Afraid he was going to suggest going to his office—the last place she wanted to be right now—she almost sagged in relief when he motioned toward the door of the exam room Claire had just vacated. Maybe he felt the same reluctance to share his office space with her. Fine, as far as she was concerned.

She swept through the doorway ahead of him, grabbing up a few items and starting to stow them away. The snick of the lock stopped her cold. Swinging around to face him, her eyes went to the door, which was indeed locked. What was that all about?

"I didn't think you wanted anyone to overhear this particular discussion."

He was right. Stella already knew too much, and she didn't know the half of it. "Thanks."

His chest rose as he took a deep breath. "About yesterday…"

"It's fine. Just call it a combination of exhaustion and sleep deprivation. We were both half-asleep at the time."

One corner of his mouth quirked up. "Are you sure about that?"

"About being exhausted?"

"No, about being half-asleep." The low rumble of his voice curled her toes. "Because I seem to remember you being very much awake."

The image of just how awake she'd been swept over her.

Her face heated, and her teeth clamped down on her lower lip. Maybe she should be a little more careful about choosing her words in the future. She drew a careful breath. "Well, regardless, it won't happen again."

He took a step closer. "Sometimes once is all it takes."

Her mouth opened, her brain working furiously to figure out what he was referring to, because it almost seemed like he was about to say he… "Once is all it takes to what?"

Only a foot separated them now and, try as she

may, she couldn't stop the sudden pounding of her pulse in her temples as she waited for his answer.

He reached out and slid his fingers under her chin, searching her eyes. "We didn't use any protection."

Protection. Protection. *Protection.* She finally got what he was saying, and suddenly realized why he'd been so very upset after they'd finished. They'd had sex without using a condom. He, evidently, *had* realized the implications almost immediately.

"I'm sure it's fine." Uh-huh. That's what she'd been telling herself all day, right?

"If it ends up not being…fine, you'll let me know, won't you?"

A wash of tears appeared from nowhere, and she fought not to blink, hoping they'd drain right back down her tear ducts. She wanted this pregnancy so badly, and hearing Greg talk about it in those terms made her insides spasm. What was she supposed to do, turn her hopes into a plea for the insemination to fail…to lose this chance at being a mother?

No. She drew herself up straight. "Not necessary."

"Oh, but it is, Hannah." The words were soft, but a thread of steel ran through them. His brown eyes bored into hers. "If you end up pregnant, I want to know."

She tugged away from him, her arms going around her waist as if holding whatever was inside her in place. "The situation might be a little more complicated than you think."

CHAPTER SIX

Complicated?

How could the situation possibly be any more complicated than it already was? Greg had already resigned himself to doing the right thing if Hannah became pregnant. He'd do right by the child, be a part of its life where he could—but even the thought of that made his chest tighten. One careless slip-up and he found himself at the end of a dark tunnel with the distant roar of a freight train sounding at the other end.

Hell.

He was tired, hungry and the last thing he wanted to do right now was stand in an exam room and talk about responsibility. But having this conversation in his office was out of the question. He hadn't been in there since last night, and one glimpse of those pencils scattered over the floor would do him in. He'd eventually have to go in and pick them up, a task he wasn't sure he was up to, even if he was all alone in the clinic. Knowing Hannah was somewhere nearby would make it that much worse.

He could always ask her to transfer—find her a position at another oncologist's office. But that would be copping out. And he had never turned his back on his responsibilities. Besides, she was damned good at her job. He didn't want to lose her, if he didn't have to.

"Do you have any plans for this evening?" he asked, when she continued to stand there without explaining what she meant by her words.

"I'm sorry?" The hint of panic in her eyes made his gut churn. Surely she didn't think he was coming on to her. Again. This would be a good time to knock that notion right out of the ballpark and let it stay there. There would be no repeats. "I mean, it's almost seven, and I haven't eaten. I'm guessing you haven't either."

"No."

No, she hadn't eaten? Or, no, she didn't want to get anything with him?

"Are you up for grabbing a bite? We can talk on the way."

She hesitated before giving a simple nod.

Halfway to the Seafood Bistro, about five miles from his office, he still hadn't opened his mouth and tackled the subject at hand. And neither had she. Instead, she stared pensively out the window, her right elbow propped on the window ledge of the vehicle, chin cupped in her palm. She'd avoided looking at him since he'd cornered her at the clinic, except when he'd taken hold of her and forced her eyes to his in the hallway. Was it better to talk now, or after his dinner had time to sink to the bottom of his stomach like a rock?

Tightening his fingers around the wheel, he glanced over at her. "Okay, we both agree this situation is complicated. So what are we going to do about it?"

She shrugged, still not looking his way. "I suggest we adopt a watch-and-wait attitude."

Watch and wait? He was an oncologist so, yes, there were times when it was wise to sit back and see what happened. But other times you had to plan ahead, take aggressive measures before things got out of hand.

Like what? Exactly what kind of measures could he take, besides setting up some kind of trust fund? And there was no way he'd ask her to get an abortion. His chest tightened even as the thought went through his mind.

Would she, if the opportunity presented itself?

Complicated was right.

So, maybe he could start with a trust fund, although he chafed at the idea of something so impersonal. Sticking a sizeable sum in an account once a month seemed cold and distant, hardly the kind of "taking responsibility" he'd talked about earlier.

His sister would have frowned at him for even considering it, would have said he was taking the easy way out. Just like when his father had wanted him to skip college in order to take over the family business. Greg had been on the verge of giving up his dreams, until Bethany had dropped the application for medical school on his bed and told him to do what was right, not what was easy.

Time to do the right thing.

"How long do you intend to wait before verifying things?"

She finally turned and looked at him. "You didn't get me pregnant, Greg, I'm almost sure of it, okay?"

"Almost sure doesn't cut it, in this situation."

"It's possible my body is still so messed up from the chemo that I won't be able to conceive. Ever. So I hardly think one quickie is going to do the trick."

Quickie. Okay, that stung. Even if she'd been as quick as he had.

And, damn it, he'd tried to do the right thing then, too, had tried to stop and get a condom. He hadn't just thrown caution to the wind. Was she really so sure that she couldn't get pregnant?

"Have you talked to a doctor about your fertility?"

Her elbow came off the window, her hands clasping together in her lap. "Yes."

"And what did he say?"

There was a long pause before she answered. "*She* said there are no guarantees."

The soft wistfulness in her voice made him sad, even while he physically relaxed into his seat. Maybe the situation wasn't the tragedy he was making it out to be. Although something inside him mourned for Hannah. They'd both known at the beginning of her treatment that the drugs could render her infertile. But when your life is at stake, you do what you have to do to give yourself the best possible outcome.

He took the turn-off to the restaurant and tried to think. They could always watch and wait, like Hannah suggested. But he really needed her to know he was there for her if she needed him. Just like his sister had been there for him.

The parking lot was just starting to fill up. Greg found an empty spot and switched off the engine, trying to decide what to do. Just then a rumble came from Hannah's seat. He blinked. "Was that your stomach?"

She gave a quick laugh. "Sorry. I think it knows we're here."

With that, the decision was made. Any further conversation could wait until she'd at least gotten something into her system. "I keep telling you, you don't have to work the same hours I do."

She stepped out of the car and waited for him to join her. "You were in surgery, and we had patients scheduled."

And Greg was normally responsible for scheduling them, which made him feel like a first-class heel. He knew he'd have to spend the day in surgery from time to time, and yet he still scheduled himself till he was up to his eyeballs in patients. In the past, he hadn't had a PA and could do his own thing—they'd simply juggled patients on days he had an emergency come up. But as his practice grew, he found himself pulled in too many directions. Hannah being available had been a godsend. One he'd taken advantage of. Maybe too much.

"Sorry, I should have kept track better. I'll try to cut back on the workload."

She touched his arm. "I like working. I want to keep doing it right up until I…" Her voice trailed away, eyes widening.

Was she planning on quitting? "Until you what?"

She hesitated. "I have something to tell you, but it can wait until after we eat."

And let him worry about it the entire meal? No. Not happening.

"Are you leaving the practice?" If she was, he wanted to know it now. Up front. Except even the thought made something in his chest dive toward his gut. Dammit. It would be easier for everyone if she did leave.

"No, not unless you want me to, or…" She blinked a couple of times. "Please, let's talk about this once we've both had something to eat. Maybe I can figure out how to say it by then."

Great. Now he was imagining all kinds of scenarios. Was she involved with someone?

Hell, he hadn't even thought about that. It would make what he'd done ten times worse. Was that the complication she'd been talking about? Had he just ruined something between her and a significant other?

Her quick glance toward the restaurant said she was serious about eating first and talking later. He remembered her stomach growling and cursed himself again. He was handling this whole situation like an idiot. No wonder he steered clear of relationships. Not only did he not have the time but he was doing a terrible job of moving this conversation in the right direction. "Okay, after we eat. But we are going to talk."

Once they were seated at the table, the server took their order and brought a cutting board loaded with a fresh loaf of pumpernickel bread. Greg nodded toward it. "Help yourself."

Hannah sliced a generous hunk and slathered it with butter. She bit into the bread with a groan, a tiny crumb landing on the outside corner of her lip. A quick flick of her tongue swept it away again.

He swallowed hard, even though his mouth was currently empty, because all he could think about was the hot kissing they'd done in the reception area of the clinic, the way she'd coaxed him into her mouth, had kept him there with the same kind of noises she was currently making. And how all he wanted to do was drag her off to some dark corner and do it all over again. This time going a hell of a lot slower.

A perfect way to repeat the same mistakes.

"Try some," she said, holding out the knife. "It's soft and very delicious."

Just like Hannah was.

He took the knife and was somehow able to hack off a chunk of bread. Shoving it into his mouth before anything he said tipped her off as to his thoughts, he chewed then swallowed.

He could have been eating shoe leather for all he knew—he couldn't taste a thing.

"Don't you like butter?"

Okay, so maybe that was why he'd had to choke it down.

She cut another piece and buttered it, then handed it to him. "It's honey butter. Try it."

Greg already knew what it tasted like, he'd been to this particular restaurant many times before, but he couldn't resist taking it from her and biting into it as she watched him. This time, he forced himself to taste the food, to let the flavors swirl on his tongue.

"Isn't it wonderful?"

His eyes held hers. "Yes. Very."

Neither of them moved or talked for the next

few seconds as they stared at each other. Then the waiter came over, and the soft clinking of a plate being set down in front of him dragged his attention away from her.

Except he didn't want this food. He wanted her to keep buttering his bread and watching him as he ate it. Wanted her to keep watching as he leaned across the table and put his lips to hers.

Greg closed his eyes and tried to force the image away. They had a serious situation on their hands. Kissing was the last thing they needed to do. So they'd eat. Have their little conversation, then he would drop her off and drive away. Intact. With a contingency plan in place in case the unthinkable actually happened.

The only thing was, he hadn't the foggiest idea what that plan was. Maybe it would come to him as he ate.

He'd ordered the fresh grilled salmon, while Hannah had claimed she was throwing caution to the wind and having the seafood Alfredo. Despite the weight she'd put on since her chemo, she was still more slender than she'd been a year ago—her hip bones had pressed into his abdomen as they'd ground together…

And that—he rotated his neck to relieve the

growing tightness in his spine—was not something he should be remembering. Not now. Not tomorrow. Not ever.

"Are you involved with someone?"

He wasn't quite sure where the words had come from, but the effect was immediate. She froze, her fork and its burden of creamy noodles stopping halfway to her mouth. "I'm sorry?"

"If I've made things awkward between you and a boyfriend, I want to apologize."

"A boyfriend?" She set her fork down and leaned forward, eyes flashing. "You think I would have... done what we did if I'd been seeing someone?"

The words, although soft, rang between them like a gong, and he immediately wished he could take back his question.

"I didn't think you were, but what happened wasn't planned. It was so sudden... I just wanted to make sure that's not what you meant by complicated."

She nodded, her lips still tight. "It's not. And since you seem so determined to do this now, I'll just come right out with it." Her fingers curled around the edge of the table. "I had an I.U.I. done yesterday morning."

"An..." His brain scrambled to find the words

that went with the acronym. Found it. "Intrauterine insemination?"

"Shh." She glanced around. "Yes."

She was *trying* to get pregnant? "Are you taking fertility drugs?"

She nodded again, her fingers now toying with the tablecloth.

Which could explain why she'd seemed so eager for him last night. The hormones tended to up the libido. That might be the reason for *her* reaction, but what about his? He seemed to be a walking commercial for Viagra whenever she was around.

Something else occurred to him. She'd said her system could be so messed up that she might not be able to conceive. If she'd had an I.U.I. that morning, surely she hadn't been trying to up her odds of getting pregnant by sleeping with him.

Hannah wouldn't do that. Would she?

"How badly do you want a pregnancy?"

"What do you mean?"

"That wasn't what last night was about, was it?"

If he'd thought his question about a significant other had raised her hackles, this one had done that times ten, if the angry color marching along her cheekbones was anything to go by. "I think I'd like to leave now."

When she reached for her purse, he put his hand over hers. "Don't. I don't know why I asked that. I just had no idea you wanted to… The timing seems so…"

"Convenient?"

"Yes." A sense of shame washed over him the second he admitted it. "But I should have known better."

"I can see how it might look but, I promise you, I didn't want what happened any more than you did."

Complicated. She'd hit that word on the head.

He nodded toward her food. "Go ahead and eat, Hannah, before it gets cold."

"I'd rather just get this over with, okay? I didn't use you to boost my chances. But even if I am pregnant, there's no way to know if it's yours or the donor's. Let's just leave it alone."

He took his hand off hers. "There's always D.N.A. testing."

"I won't go that route. Not before the baby—if there even is a baby—is born. I won't take that risk, especially since the fertility specialist couldn't promise the I.U.I. would even work. If it does, I don't want to lose it. I might never get another opportunity to have a baby. Let's just assume that the donor's…er contribution is the only player in the game. It had at least a twelve-hour head start."

She was handing him an easy way out, one he should grab with both hands. But his sister's face appeared before him, that little furrow cutting between her brows. This time he didn't need the warning, however. Something in him wanted to know if the child was his. He wouldn't be able to look at Hannah's growing body without wondering. And he'd have a hard time looking at himself in the mirror if he closed his eyes and pretended none of this had ever happened.

"What about after it's born? You can have the testing done then. It's as easy as swabbing the inside of the child's cheek."

"Why bother, Greg? No matter whose D.N.A. the baby carries, I'll be the one raising it, nurturing it. That's what I wanted when I started down this road. It's still what I want. This was my decision. Not yours."

A flush of anger crept through him, growing stronger as he realized what she was saying. So much for taking responsibility for his actions. Hannah was going to try to shut him out completely.

"That's where you're wrong," he said, fixing his attention on those gorgeous green eyes of hers.

"It may have started out as your decision, but that changed the moment we had unprotected sex." She flinched at those words, but he kept going. "I was as much a part of that particular decision as you were. If this child is the result of our coming together—no matter the hows or whys—then it won't be just *your* baby. It'll be mine, as well."

CHAPTER SEVEN

Snow.

Hannah scrunched her nose when she pulled aside the drapes. It was just a light dusting of the stuff, and she'd seen worse in October. Much worse. But dark skies promised more of the same. She'd hoped winter might hold off a little longer.

She glanced over at the rustic wooden settle she'd made a couple of years ago, just before her illness. Hopefully her red ice grippers were still inside the storage area beneath it and would hold up for one more winter. She'd have to dig them out and make sure. Although how much hiking she'd get in this year was yet to be seen. But if she wound up pregnant, they could come in handy as she grew larger and weather conditions began to deteriorate. Walking across an icy parking lot to the grocery store was treacherous enough even when her center of gravity wasn't pushed forward by a foot.

Her work schedule was still busy, although, true to his word, Greg had cut back on the number of patients they saw after six o'clock. At least on days he was scheduled to be at the hospital. All other days, he continued working like a crazy person.

She sighed. It had been a week since they'd had their last big discussion, when he'd insisted he wanted a role in the baby's life, if there was a baby and if it ended up being his.

How? She barely saw him during office hours these days, and she worked with the man. How did he expect to make time for a baby? Was that really the role model she wanted for a child? That of a workaholic whose job came before everything else?

To be fair, he was helping a lot of people, and he was right when he'd said she hadn't complained when she'd been on the receiving end of that help. But Greg had never had to face the harsh reality that life didn't go on forever. It was up to each person to make the most of their time on earth.

He was certainly doing that by giving back to those around him, but what about his own life? When did he start living? Really living?

Maybe he hadn't really meant his offer—maybe it was just the obligatory "take responsibility for your actions" spiel that faded away once the guilt loosened its hold.

Hannah swallowed. She'd seen the look in his eye, had heard the quiet anger in his voice after she'd insisted the baby was hers alone.

What a mess.

And it was Saturday. Not even a day when she could throw herself into work and not have time to think. Her pregnancy test that morning had yielded nothing, which didn't necessarily mean the I.U.I. had failed. Her doctor said it was better to test at the two-week mark, but she hadn't been able to wait.

What if she wasn't pregnant?

While it should be a relief to know she couldn't possibly be carrying Greg's child—and that she'd be able to have another procedure done after her next cycle—she couldn't convince her heart it was for the best.

Sigh.

She turned away from the window and headed for the kitchen, where she had a batch of sunshine muffins baking. A perfect foil for the gloomy day. The wonderful scent of citrus washed over her as she dug her oven mitt from one of the drawers. Peeking inside the oven, she noted the muffins were just starting to set, their swollen tops curving over the edge of the pan, like twelve pregnant little bellies.

Great, was this what she was in for? Picturing her future body at every turn?

Just as she pulled the muffin tray out of the oven, the phone chirped. She dropped the pan onto the stovetop and hurried into the living room, tugging the mitt from her hand as she went.

"Hello?"

"Hannah Lassiter, please."

The brisk voice stopped her cold because she immediately recognized it. Greg. Why on earth was he calling her at home on a Saturday morning? "Th-this is Hannah."

"I know it is. Habit. Sorry."

What was a habit? Asking for the person, even when you knew who it was? Her heart took a dive when she realized why he was calling. "Where are you?"

"At the office. I've had an emergency come up and need to pull some records off the computer. I already tried calling Stella, but nobody's home."

"Is the computer on?"

"No. I can't find the damn power button on the system."

"It's on the front of the tower, under the reception desk."

"I've already tried pushing that and nothing happened."

She licked her lips. Oh, no. That thing could be ornery at times. "Try it again."

There was a pause, and then a low curse. "Still nothing."

"I'll be there in a few minutes." Was she crazy? True, she'd just been complaining about having nothing to do, but this wasn't quite what she'd had in mind.

There was a lengthy pause over the phone. "Greg? Are you still there?"

"I'm here. If I could just reach Stella… You don't happen to have the number to her cell, do you? It's not on the pad with the other numbers."

"No, sorry. It might be in the personnel records, but those would be on the computer, as well. The system's temperamental. Stella showed me a few tricks, so hang tight."

"I don't want you to have to come in."

Hannah could pretty much swear he didn't want her anywhere around, since he'd steered clear of her as much as possible over the last week. "If it's an emergency, I don't mind. Who is it?"

"Claire Taylor. Her husband thinks she's having a reaction to the chemo and wants me to take a look."

Oh, no. The breast-cancer patient she'd seen a week ago. "Are they headed in now?"

"Yes."

"I'm on my way." Before he could hand her any more arguments, she pressed End, cutting off anything he'd been about to say.

She ran to the bedroom and threw on the nearest set of scrubs she found. How was it that more than half her wardrobe was made up of the comfortable clothes? She even slept in a clean set most of the time.

Giving her hair a quick brush, she shoved a plastic headband up over her forehead so she wouldn't have to blow-dry her bangs into any semblance of order. She decided to forgo makeup as well, in the interests of time—resisting the little voice inside her that urged her to make an effort. Neither Greg nor the patient cared how she looked. She'd stay long enough to get that computer system up and running, then she'd take off again. Fifteen minutes in and out, tops.

The image of her and Greg and their quick "in

and out" session ran through her head and she groaned aloud. *Stop it.*

As she ran back through the kitchen, she grabbed a canvas grocery bag and slid the entire tray of muffins inside. She could eat in the car as she was starving. And since Greg's call had come in just after eight o'clock, she doubted he'd fixed himself much of a breakfast either. He'd probably been at the office for at least a half hour, fiddling with that computer, before being forced to call for help. Besides, there was no way she could eat a dozen muffins by herself. She'd leave some there for him to take home.

The trip to the clinic took less than ten minutes. Thankfully the light snow hadn't turned into ice, so the roads were clear and dry so far. She hadn't gotten a chance to listen to the forecast, so she could only hope the weather held until she got out of there.

She found the front door to the clinic unlocked, so she pushed through it, muffins in one hand, purse in the other. Greg popped up from behind the desk, where he'd evidently still been trying to figure out the computer. His eyes skimmed over her and he blinked a couple of times.

Did she look that bad? Because he sure didn't.

His hair was sticking up a bit, probably from dragging his fingers through it in frustration as she'd seen him do many times before. He was more casual today in a dark T-shirt that hugged his chest and arms.

Setting her things on the counter so she didn't end up staring, she slid the muffin pan from the bag. "Here, eat."

He stood the rest of the way, and she noted that his lower half was as casual as the upper. Worn jeans gripped his lean hips and thighs, the color fading where the fabric followed a certain decadent curve. One that had her biting her lip in an effort to rip her gaze away from it.

A throat cleared, the sound shocking her back into action. "What are they?"

They? Oh, the food.

"Sunshine muffins. They have pineapple and orange zest. They're happy tasting."

His lips curved as he took the napkin-wrapped muffin she held out. "I don't think I've ever heard anyone refer to food as 'happy.'"

"Wait until you taste one." She took a muffin for herself, realizing she hadn't eaten in the car as she'd intended.

Greg's white teeth cut the miniature cake in half,

his brows going up. He swallowed and then studied the muffin. "Okay, so maybe there's something to that description."

"Told you." She took a bite of her own piece, loving the way the pineapple chunks provided a little extra spurt of moisture. Anyone who'd ever eaten these knew they were about as close to heaven as you could get.

She swallowed. Well, she used to believe that. Up until a week ago.

"Well, I'll see about that computer." Taking her muffin with her, she edged past Greg, who'd finished his first one and was reaching for a second.

"Thanks for these. I forgot to eat."

Just as she'd suspected. Kneeling in front of the computer, she took another bite as she felt around the back of the CPU box and jiggled one of the many cords snaking behind the equipment to make sure it was tight in its slot.

She pressed the power button and heard the promising whine of success.

"It's coming up." Greg's voice came from beside her and, as she knew they would, her eyes paused as they traveled up his leg—even though it was obvious he was talking about the computer monitor coming up and not something else.

Gawd. What was wrong with her? Wasn't she in enough trouble as it was?

She forced herself to look at his face. "Come here, and I'll show you what to do the next time it happens."

The second he crouched beside her, she realized asking him to do so had been a huge mistake. Ducked down behind the desk together, their knees touched, making the space seem smaller and much more intimate.

She held up the attached cord, horrified to note it shook in time with her hand. "This one comes loose periodically. Stella says that if you bump it the wrong way, it shuts everything off. The thing drives her crazy."

"I'll have to have it fixed," he murmured. "Where does the cord lead?"

His fingers touched hers for a second before sliding along the piece of wiring, her heart crashing around in her chest as the scent of soap and cool aftershave hit her senses. She could lean three inches to the left and her cheek would slide along his jaw. She forced her body to go rigid instead and held her ground.

"Ah, there you are." He withdrew his hand and turned to look at her, their faces now inches apart.

"So all I need to do is make sure there's a good connection?"

"C-connection?" Her brain struggled with the word, since the only connection she could think of involved having her lips mashed up against his. "Oh, the power cable."

"What did you think I was talking about?" His voice was impossibly low, his breath gliding across her cheek.

He didn't want to know.

"The computer, of course."

"Ah, and here I thought you were talking about matches."

As in the "playing with matches" comment she'd made a week ago?

His lips curved with a secret knowledge. He knew exactly what she'd been thinking.

"Hannah." The chiding tone should have made her smile back, but it didn't.

Instead, the tip of her tongue came out to moisten her mouth just as Greg's fingers walked up her nape then curved around it, the warmth of his hand sending a shiver over her.

Lord, was he going to kiss her? Again?

The sudden tinkle of the bell over the front door made Hannah rear back so quickly she landed on her backside with a grunt. She then jumped up from behind the desk, her hand automatically going to her hair as if she'd just been caught doing something naughty. Which she hadn't. At least, not yet.

It was the patient and her husband. She could only hope that Greg had crawled away on his hands and knees and made his escape, because if he stood up right now...

As if on cue, her boss unfolded his long length and casually climbed to his feet, brushing dust from the front of jeans, while she cringed inwardly.

He came around the counter, and offered his hand to each of them. "One of our computer connections seemed to have come loose, and I couldn't switch it on. Hannah was showing me which cable it was."

Not a tremor or a warble affected his voice, and even Hannah believed him. What he'd said was true, after all. So why did her face burn like the inside of a kiln? Because her boss could quite possibly be the father of her child? And she'd been about to let him try for a double. Ack!

In the background, she heard Greg asking about Claire's symptoms in low, soothing tones. By now they were all seated in the waiting room's leatherette chairs, with Greg leaning forward as if trying to catch every word his patient said.

Hannah could remember him doing exactly the same thing when he'd visited her in the hospital that first time. He hadn't written anything down, instead he'd let her pour out all her hopes and fears and had answered each of her questions. A little black book had sat in his lap, but he'd never opened it until the very end, when he'd scheduled her appointment.

That appointment book was nowhere in sight right now, but she had no doubt Greg would remember everything spoken in that room.

She wasn't sure what to do. Did he want her to leave now that the computer problem had been fixed? She could at least look up Claire's chart, as that's what he'd wanted the computer for in the first place. She sat behind the desk and flipped through screens until she came to the patient's information. Hitting Print, she went over and retrieved the small stack of papers that contained digitized test results and observations. Then she padded over to Greg, who held out a hand for the packet without taking his eyes off his patient.

"I want to take a look and see what's going on,

okay?" He glanced at the woman's husband. "Why don't you come back with us?"

A wave of relief washed over her. She could escape while everyone was in the back.

Right before Greg walked through the door, he glanced back. "Would you mind waiting around for a while? I could really use another of those muffins."

A muffin? He really expected her to believe that?

"Um…no, not at all. I'll be happy to stay."

As soon as he left, Hannah sank into a chair, leaning her head against the cream-colored wall behind her with a roll of her eyes. She'd be happy to stay? Why hadn't she just said, "And where would you like me this time, sir? In your office? Or shall we climb back under the front desk?"

Greg wasn't sure why he'd asked Hannah to stay, other than to find out if she'd heard anything about her hormone levels. Had her HCG spiked? Or remained level?

His patient lay on the exam table, her husband murmuring softly to her. She looked so remarkably like his sister that he often found himself staring as if she could suddenly morph into Bethany at any moment and start laughing about old times.

Even the eternal spark of optimism was something his sister had had. He was convinced that if Bethany had lived, she would have turned out very much like Claire—a kind, giving, cheerful person. She would have had a happy life…had a husband who adored her, just as Claire's husband obviously doted on his wife.

Watching the pair, he saw nothing of the grasping greediness he'd felt when he had gone after his PA last week.

There was so much he should regret about that night, but he couldn't seem to wring that particular emotion from his brain, or any other part of his body. Instead, he had been ready to move in for another sample just before his patient had walked through the door.

Luckily she had, because seeing her had snapped him back to the present and reminded him exactly why he was there. Especially when he saw how pale she was, how tired looking. He hadn't been able to save his sister, but he was damned well going to do everything in his power to help Claire. Was he using his patient as a substitute? Doing for one what he hadn't been able to do for the other? Maybe, but in the end it didn't matter as long as it worked.

He forced his attention back to Claire. He could have asked Hannah to come in with him, but he needed a little breathing space. Besides, taking blood pressure and temperature gave him something concrete to do with his hands, and with his thoughts.

He glanced at the readout on the tympanic thermometer and frowned. One hundred point one degrees. A low-grade fever. The beginning of an infection? Not good when dealing with a chemo patient's weakened immune system. A thread of worry twisted inside him. "Have you been exposed to anyone who's ill?"

"I don't think so. I had chills last night, and stomach cramps. I had a little fever, but nothing too terrible."

He felt her abdomen for signs of tenderness. "Does anything hurt right now?"

"No. I actually feel better, but Doug insisted on calling."

Good man. He nodded at him in reassurance.

"And he was right. You still have a slight fever. I'm going to prescribe some antibiotics, just in case, but if your temperature climbs above one hundred and two degrees, I want you call me and then head straight to Anchorage Regional and let them give you some intravenous meds."

Her husband placed his hand on her shoulder. "Do you want her to do her chemo treatment this week?"

"When's it scheduled?"

"Friday morning."

Almost a week away. She needed to stay on the regimen if at all possible. "If her fever's gone completely, then go ahead, as long as her blood count looks good." He glanced back at his patient. "Can I check the incision?"

He knew this was hard for her, but he had to be sure nothing was acting up.

Claire swallowed, but opened the gown so that he could check the mastectomy site for signs of redness or infection. Her husband held her hand and leaned down to whisper in her ear again while Greg studied the area. It looked clean and well healed. Her pulled her robe closed and gently squeezed her shoulder. "I don't see anything here to worry about."

Grabbing a pad from a nearby drawer, he scribbled a prescription for antibiotics.

Claire spoke up. "Sorry to drag you away from whatever you were doing."

It took him a second to realize she was talking in generalities and not about catching him and Hannah under the figurative boardwalk. Being able drop everything at a moment's notice to help patients like Claire was the exact reason he'd chosen not to have a wife and family. His sister had stayed on his case until he'd agreed to at least try med school for a year. She'd been right. He was meant to be a doctor.

His throat tightened. She hadn't lived to see the completion of that dream. But he could honor her memory by being the best damned doctor he could be. Especially since the doctor who'd ultimately treated her during her illness had been everything he'd learned to despise in a physician. He'd cared more about his golf swing than his patients.

Maybe that wasn't an entirely fair assessment, but that particular specialist's reputation—as he'd discovered later—left a little to be desired.

"Don't apologize. I wasn't doing anything special today. And I always want you to call if something's worrying you. It's usually easier to head problems off than to try to fix them once the wheels have been spinning for a while."

He helped her sit up and handed her the prescription.

"Thank you. Your patients are lucky," she said.

He smiled. Luck had nothing to do with it. If she wanted to thank anyone, she should thank his sister. Without her, he wouldn't be where he was today. He'd be on a commercial fishing boat, freezing his ass off and hating life. Instead, he was doing a job he loved—one that gave him immense satisfaction.

For that reason and a myriad of others, Greg had fashioned his practice differently than most oncologists. He hired people whose lives had been touched by cancer. Survivors. He found it was the best way to keep his head clear of distractions and fixed on the task at hand. And helped him remember his sister.

And it had worked. At least until Hannah had come along. Her murmurs of concern had worn him down little by little, until he'd thrown himself on the rocks, just as sailors of old had when confronted with the sirens' song.

He went into the hallway to wait for his patient to get dressed, knowing that as inwardly battered and bruised as he might be right now, he was eventually going to have to walk into that waiting room and face down temptation all over again.

CHAPTER EIGHT

"CONGRATULATIONS, Hannah, you're pregnant."

The fertility doctor's voice confirmed what her own home pregnancy test had indicated. She was carrying someone's baby.

But whose?

Be happy, Hannah. This is what you wanted.

It was. But not like this. Where she'd anticipated the ability to raise her child as she saw fit, sharing her newfound zest for life, dread had oozed in, infecting her happiness. The fact that she couldn't wholeheartedly celebrate this moment made her angry. Angry at Greg, but even more angry at herself.

Why was he so persistent?

I want to know if this baby is mine, one way or the other. I don't care how long it takes to find out.

His parting words last Saturday echoed through her head. He'd asked her to wait at the clinic until he'd finished examining Claire, but when he'd finally emerged, keys in hand, he hadn't mentioned the muffins, confirming her suspicions that it had merely been a way to get her to stay. Instead, he'd made that statement before holding the door open and watching her walk toward her car. Once she had been safely inside, engine on, heat cranked up, he'd turned away to lock the clinic door.

And that had been it.

They'd passed each other in the hallway this week, but neither had said much to the other. The clinic was busy, although, true to Greg's word, the overall hours remained shorter. Hannah had her suspicions about that, too, as he stayed behind every night. Notes added to certain patients' files upped those suspicions. He was seeing more patients after hours.

That brought her back to her original question. Why was he so insistent on knowing whose child this was, when he wouldn't have time to spend with it? There was no way she wanted to introduce a two-year-old to a man and tell him or her, "This is your father," only to have Greg continue on with his life as he'd always done. That was not the message she wanted to send to her child: you're not important enough for Daddy to spend time with.

God. What a disaster.

"Hannah, did you hear me?" The fertility doctor touched her shoulder, making her jump.

She glanced up, seeing the concern on the woman's face. "Sorry. That's wonderful news."

"Then why don't you sound ecstatic?"

"It's complicated." As soon as the words came out of her mouth, she snorted in disgust. That seemed to be her new favorite phrase. "Let me ask you something. Is it possible to do D.N.A. testing before the baby's birth?"

Dr. Chaquir leaned against the cabinet behind her. "Is there something I should know? A genetic problem in your family?"

Another thing Hannah had never thought of when she'd had sex with her boss. Was he carrying some kind of defect? Was that why he was so fired up about knowing one way or the other? Surely he'd have said something before now.

No. Why would he? If the child wasn't his, he had no reason to tell her anything.

Her hand went to her stomach as if she could protect the tiny fetus from some kind of horrible problem. Maybe she did need to find out.

She sighed. "I…um, did something stupid."

The doctor frowned. "How stupid?"

"Stupid enough to not know if this baby is the result of donor sperm or someone else's."

"I don't see how. Unless you were with someone immediately afterward, I'm pretty sure the donor sperm reached the egg first."

"But the life cycle of washed sperm is shorter than…um, the other kind, right?"

Dr. Chaquir nodded. "Six to twenty-four hours on average, compared with up to five days for fresh ejaculate. I'm taking it you were intimate not long after the I.U.I. was performed?"

Hannah's face heated. "Within that time frame you mentioned."

There was a pause. "I see."

Those two words told her all she needed to know. The doctor was not going to heave a dramatic sigh and say, "You lucky thing, it's definitely not your boss's baby."

"So, as far as prenatal D.N.A. testing goes, how risky is it?"

"You're going to want to talk with your OB/GYN about that." She paused. "Are you sure you want to go through with this pregnancy, Hannah? It's still pretty early."

Did she?

Yes. This was her baby. The one she'd dreamed

of as she'd sat in the recliner in the chemo room, having toxic substances pumped into her veins. The "happy place" she'd traveled to during some of the unpleasant side effects. This was something she'd wanted more than anything, and she might never get another chance.

"Yes, I want to go through with it." She forced a smile and stood. "Thank you, Doctor. If you could give me a referral for an obstetrician, I'd appreciate it."

On the drive back home, a sudden rush of joy—in the form of tears—dumped whatever dread she'd felt right out of her body. She pulled off the side of the road as moisture cascaded down her cheeks. The bad emotions might come back soon enough, but right now she could celebrate. She *would* celebrate.

She was pregnant. *Pregnant!*

No matter what came next, she would soon hold a new being in her arms and glory in the miracle of modern medicine that made it possible. Maybe some deity had seen how badly she wanted this and had sent Greg to her at just the right time. What did it matter?

She scrubbed at her cheeks. Okay, so it did matter. A lot. But she could deal with that later, once the reality sank deep and she had to face Greg with the news. But for now it was Friday afternoon and she didn't have to face anyone for the next two days. Not until Monday morning. By then she'd have come up with the perfect words to toss at Greg.

"Any news?"

Greg had come up behind her silently, and she gave a muffled scream before whirling around to face him. "When did you get here?"

"About an hour ago."

Her two-day search for a quick and easy answer had been fruitless. She'd come up with zilch. Maybe even less than zilch. Because she'd dreamed of herself—very pregnant—in a flowing wedding gown on Saturday night and when she reached the altar, the faceless groom had yanked a sign from beneath his tuxedo coat that read, "Is that my baby?"

She'd awoken in a cold sweat, unsure if the accusing figure represented the sperm donor or Greg.

She turned her attention back to the man in front of her, whose face was very real and who was asking much the same thing as the groom from her dream. Only she didn't have a better answer now than she'd had then.

"Yes. I found out on Friday."

"You're pregnant." He'd evidently seen the truth on her face.

"Yes."

He leaned a shoulder against the wall as if needing the extra bit of support. "So what do we do now?"

Hannah glanced to her left, hoping Stella wasn't going to suddenly pop out of one of the exam rooms. "I have an appointment to see an obstetrician in a couple of weeks."

"Will you ask for testing?"

"I'm going to ask *about* testing." In her mind, asking for information was very different from asking to have it done. "I'm really not holding you responsible, Greg. It was a fluke, something neither of us expected to happen. Please, can't you just leave it at that?"

His jaw tightened. "You might not hold me responsible, but I do. I knew what the consequences could be, knew I had a condom in the wallet not five feet away from me. I went ahead without it."

As opposed to her, who hadn't thought about anything but having him inside her as soon as possible. A condom had never even crossed her mind, maybe because in her head she had already been pregnant, which was ridiculous. If this was anyone's fault, it was probably hers. "I was there, too. I didn't exactly give you the opportunity to stop."

Something dark flickered through his eyes before it winked back out. "I could have handled the whole situation differently—never let it go as far as it did."

How? By shoving her away when she'd reached for him? That would have been the ultimate humiliation. Even worse than having to stand here now and hear him imply that had been one of the options.

"Knowing the truth isn't going to change anything. Not really. You live to work. I live…to live. Like it or not, cancer changed me. I don't expect you to be able to understand that, but I want to share what I've been given with others. That includes my child. I want it to know my hopes and dreams. To teach it the same values I have. I want the baby to know how precious each and every second of life is."

He folded his arms across his chest and waited as a nurse made her way past them. "You don't think I want those same things?"

"Quite frankly, no." She glanced pointedly in the direction the nurse had gone seconds earlier. "And I'd really like to keep the pregnancy to myself for the moment—I haven't even told my parents yet—so can we please not have this discussion in the middle of the hallway?"

Greg stared at her for a long minute. "Fine. So you tell me when and where, and I'll be there."

So much for hoping he'd walk away and leave things on some vague, undefined terms. She needed time to think about how much involvement she was willing to let Greg have. Ultimately it was her decision, but she also needed it to be the right one. She didn't want to have to explain to her child someday why she'd kept his biological father—if that turned out to be Greg—from being a part of his life. That didn't seem right either.

Maybe he was right about the D.N.A. testing. If he knew for sure the baby wasn't his, he'd stop pressuring her. And, in all honesty, he'd probably be hugely relieved to boot.

"How about you go with me to the obstetrician and hear what she has to say about the testing? I don't promise I'll have it done, if it's risky to the baby, but I don't want you to think I'm being disingenuous about anything either."

"Sounds reasonable. Let me know when the appointment is and I'll shuffle my schedule around."

She blinked in surprise. He would? Greg had never once canceled a surgery or patient's appointment since she'd worked at the clinic. Even when he was in the operating room or had an emergency with another patient, someone on the team kept the other scheduled appointments. Maybe he wasn't quite as intractable as—

Before she could finish the thought, Stella stuck her head through the door in the reception area. "The office furniture guys just called. They should be here with your new desk in around a half an hour. Will you be here to sign for it?"

Dark color washed up Greg's neck and infused his face. "Yes. I'll be here."

Stella nodded. "Oh, and one more thing, they want to know what you want done with the old one…said you mentioned something about needing it out of here as soon as possible." She paused. "Didn't you just have your office redecorated this past summer?"

"I can't remember." He pushed away from the wall and began stalking toward his office. "Let me know when they arrive."

"Will do." Stella withdrew, leaving Hannah to

stare at Greg's retreating back, humiliation and hurt jockeying for first place in her head.

That desk. The one where they'd made love.

Was it really so easy to erase what had happened between them? It evidently was for Greg. One flick of his wrist and he made the desk—and everything it represented—vanish forever.

CHAPTER NINE

"CHANCES of miscarriage are one in a hundred."

The obstetrician continued explaining how chorionic villus testing worked and what to expect during the procedure, but Greg's mind fastened on the risk factors. The phrase ran through his head time and time again.

Hannah, dressed in a standard hospital gown, sat on the exam table and listened intently to the doctor. Her face was a blank slate, giving Greg no indication of what she was thinking. Her appointment had been the first one of the day, and if Dr. Preston was surprised to see him accompanying her new patient, she didn't show it.

Greg had stepped outside the room during the internal exam but had been called back in during the explanations. Everything with the pregnancy seemed to be normal. Hannah was six weeks along, but that time was calculated from her last period, not the date of conception, which had been two weeks after that date. But, still, how had four weeks passed from the fateful encounter in his office? Time had kind of become a vague BC/AD delineation of time in which BC stood for "before condom" and AD meant "after dumbass."

Hannah had been given a tentative July due date, which seemed both way too soon and an eternity away. His life would be turned upside down until he knew for sure whether or not he was the father.

But at a one-in-a-hundred chance of losing the baby? Was his peace of mind really worth that much?

He moved closer to the exam table and touched Hannah's arm, interrupting the doctor's litany. "Don't do it."

Hannah blinked up at him. "I'm sorry?"

Her question made him realize just how far they'd traveled away from the subject of D.N.A. testing. Greg had no idea what the current topic was, but he had to make his wishes clear. "I don't want you to do the paternity testing."

The doctor glanced from one to the other. "Do you want me to give you a moment?"

"Do you mind?" Hannah's voice was soft, her eyes still on his.

"Not at all. I'll get started with my next patient."

The doctor squeezed Hannah's shoulder, gave Greg an enigmatic look and slid through the door.

"I thought you wanted the testing done," Hannah said as soon as they were alone.

"It's too risky."

"But when I mentioned that earlier, you just brushed it aside."

Greg dragged a hand through his hair. She was right, he had. He didn't know what had changed between then and now, but something had. Maybe having tangible evidence the pregnancy was real. "I think hearing the actual numbers made me rethink things. If they weren't so high…"

Where exactly was that line? If the doctor had said the chances of losing the pregnancy were one in a thousand, would he want her to have it done? One in a million?

He wasn't sure. But a hundred to one. That wasn't a risk he was willing to put Hannah through. Not for the selfish reasons he had.

"Maybe later on," she said. "An amniocentesis could carry fewer risks."

"You're not old enough to warrant testing for genetic defects." He frowned. "Unless there's something in your family."

"No. And the donor didn't list any kind of problems." She hesitated. "Is there anything in your family?"

Was there? Greg had no idea. He'd long since given up on the idea of having kids, so he'd never bothered checking his family tree for inheritable conditions. Although he seemed to remember reading that myeloid leukemia—his sister's illness—could be caused by a defective chromosome in about thirty percent of cases. Hell, something he'd never even bothered to think about. Selfish bastard. All he'd worried about were the ramifications to his own life if he were the baby's father. What about the ramifications to the child's life?

"My sister had myeloid leukemia. If I'm the father…" His voice trailed away. Hell, what if he'd passed on some kind of time bomb?

"Is myeloid inherited?"

"I think it can be." He thought about it for a second. "I'll see a geneticist and ask about testing."

Hannah's face drained of color. "Oh, God. Even if there is a test, it could take weeks or longer to get the results."

He took her hand and squeezed. "I'm so sorry. If I could take it all back, I would." He'd had strange, uneasy dreams about that night ever since. He'd wake up drenched in sweat, wanting her with a fervor that shook him. Worse was when he reached for her upon waking, only to find the other side of his bed empty. Cold.

And now this.

"It's not your fault." She gave him a shaky smile. "I've often wished that night had happened a whole lot earlier, or later. But I was taking hormones and they…well, they probably affected my thinking."

In other words, if she'd been in her right mind, she'd have never had sex with him. Fantastic. And that made him feel a whole lot better, because he had no excuse, other than having had the hots for his beautiful PA almost from the moment he'd laid eyes on her. Even as a patient, there'd been something special about her, something that drew him.

Hiring her had been a mistake. He'd felt it at the time but had figured the attraction would fade. He'd felt a twinge of lust for a woman from time to time. It never lasted. And that attraction had certainly had never made him lose his head before.

"Are you sure it wasn't just my charismatic personality that did the trick?" He'd been abrupt with her when she'd brought him coffee that fateful day. He wasn't sure making a joke was the right thing to do under these circumstances, but it was all he had.

"That was probably it." She lifted her brows and regarded him for a moment or two. "What ever happened to the desk?"

Heat sifted up Greg's neck. So she had suspected the real reason he'd swapped it. Not that it had helped. The white pickled wood—so different from the rich mahogany of the previous desk—still seemed to be burned with the image of Hannah splayed across it.

And come to think of it, she rarely ventured into his office nowadays, whereas before, hardly a day had gone by that she hadn't brought him coffee or stopped to chat about a patient. He used to be irritated by her apparent lack of boundaries, like the impulsive hug she'd given him when they'd still been patient and doctor—something his sister might have done.

His reaction to Hannah's embrace, however, had been anything but brotherly. But as much as she confused him and caused him to forget himself, he found he missed those daily visits. And as for that old desk…

"It's in storage." He hadn't quite been able to get rid of it entirely. The men had offered to haul it to a consignment shop, but he'd balked at the last second and instead rented a unit in one of the pricier, climate-controlled facilities. He figured he'd take care of it by the time the next rental payment was due.

"Oh." Hannah's face turned a delicate shade of pink. "Well, I guess I'd better get dressed. I'm sure you need to head back to the office."

"I don't have an appointment for another couple of hours." He hadn't been sure how long these initial obstetrician visits took, and he hadn't wanted to leave in the middle of it. Not that he'd even needed to be here in the first place.

Yeah, he had. He'd needed to hear the risk factors in person, and to see Hannah's reaction to them. He'd come away certain of one thing. She wanted this baby. Who was he to jeopardize that possibility?

And if he'd passed on some defective chromosome? Could he handle seeing his child go through the same thing his sister had endured somewhere down the road? He didn't think so, but that wasn't his choice to make. It was Hannah's. And he wouldn't have given up knowing his sister for anything. Her steadfast solidarity—after he told his father of his decision to go to med school—had been his rock during a time of seething turmoil and anger.

Hannah's voice cut through his thoughts. "Unless you want me to get dressed in front of you, you might want to wait outside."

Ah, okay, so that's what she'd been getting at by telling him to go back to the office. He needed to pull himself together. Something about this woman made him say and do things that were completely out of character. "Sorry. I'll…go. Out there." He jerked a thumb in the direction of the door.

"I drove, so why don't I just meet you back at the office?"

A wave of tension he hadn't even been aware of rolled off his shoulders. "Do you want me to send the doctor back in?"

"That's right. I forgot about her." She paused, her eyes going to his. "You've never talked about your sister before. Did she…?"

"She didn't make it." The sorrow from years past gathered in his throat, and he had to swallow hard.

Hannah took his hand again. "I'm so sorry. How long ago?"

"About ten years."

"So you weren't a doctor at the time?"

He sighed, not liking the way her hand wrapped around his or how natural it felt. "I was in med school when she was diagnosed. It happened faster than anyone expected." It was ironic that the very profession she'd encouraged him to pursue hadn't been able to help her in the end.

"And yet you specialized in oncology. Isn't that hard?" The compassion in her eyes was hard to face. And yet it wasn't pity, simply a deep understanding. Of course. How stupid of him. Hannah had traveled the same road as his sister, only her illness had veered down a different fork and had had a much better outcome.

"It's why I specialized. My sister was my biggest cheerleader when I decided to become a doctor. It seemed like the best way to thank her." Why he'd blurted that out, he had no idea. He'd never told anyone his reasons for going into this particular field, not even his parents—although they probably knew.

"Of course." The words were soft, carrying a hint of surprise, as if she'd just figured something out. "I need to get dressed."

She let go of his hand, leaving an emptiness in its wake that he didn't like. This was ridiculous. Even if she ended up carrying a human being that contained his D.N.A., that didn't change their relationship. He was her employer, nothing more. And he'd yet to decide what he would be to her child—

if it was even his. And that was pretty unlikely. At least he hoped it was. Because if that was the case, his life could go on unchanged, continue exactly as it had for the last ten years.

As he went through the door, he knew he was telling himself the worst kind of lie. His life—no matter what the outcome of any paternity test— would never be the same again.

"Itsy bitsy spider climbed up the water spout…"

The sing-song tune—coming from the next aisle over—was followed by the quick giggle of a child. Hannah couldn't stop her lips from curving at the cheerful sound, despite her confused jumble of thoughts about Greg, his sister's cancer and her own pregnancy.

As Greg had shared about his reasons for be-coming an oncologist, memories of her own ter-rifying struggle had roared back to life, swamping her with memories of pain and fear. Those fears had stayed with her for the past week, refusing to seep away like they normally did. Maybe because she was now responsible for someone other than herself.

She'd come into the cavernous baby supercenter on a whim, hoping to replace the bad emotions with happy ones. But standing in the middle of the store, she'd been overwhelmed by the quantity of paraphernalia surrounding her. A chaotic jumble. Just like the feelings she'd been trying to escape.

That tiny giggle did what her own frantic attempts to tame her fears couldn't: turned everything right side up so it could settle back into place. That happy laughter was why she'd wanted to get pregnant…why she was willing to go through all the doubt and uncertainty of being a single mom. She wandered over to where the sounds of singing continued and found a young mother, her dark hair shining as she leaned over a fancy baby stroller.

Hannah could almost imagine the woman's fingers walking up her child's belly as the song continued and another happy shriek filled the air, followed by the mom's light chuckle.

Hannah's smile widened. That would be her someday. At least, she hoped it would. But at the moment the thoughts of illness and fear still seemed terrifyingly real. Her hand went to her stomach, which at the seven-week point hadn't begun to expand yet. But she knew the baby was there. She might even get to hear its heartbeat at her next scheduled appointment.

In the week since her initial check-up, Greg

hadn't said anything else about his sister's illness or whether or not he'd spoken with anyone about testing, and Hannah was afraid to ask. She finally understood why he'd thrown himself headlong into his work. Doing what he hadn't been able to do for his sister. No wonder he wasn't involved with anyone. He was like a monk…someone who'd thrown aside his own creature comforts in order to seek a higher purpose in life.

And what of this child, if it was his? How could she expect Greg to change who he was? What he wanted out of life? She couldn't. Another reason she'd come into the store today.

She wanted to be able to spend a few moments not thinking about the horrible possibilities and just enjoy being pregnant—but the thoughts had followed her inside. A year ago she'd wondered if it would even be possible for her to have a baby. And yet here she was. Expecting one. The thought should make her happier than she'd ever been.

She took a deep breath and let it out slowly. Some of the tension left her. And as she watched the mother and baby interact, a sense of rightness washed over her. Nothing else mattered at the moment. She'd live for the here and now. Worrying about the future was futile, as she'd learned through her own fight. She couldn't change the outcome, could only do her best to optimize her chances for survival.

That's what she'd do for this baby, as well. She couldn't change what might or might not happen in the weeks or years to come, but she was making an effort to eat right and to do what she could to stay healthy in the present. She'd worry about the other stuff as it came up.

The mom, a few yards away, suddenly looked over her shoulder as if sensing someone was watching her. "Sorry," she said, her smile big. "I didn't realize anyone could hear me."

When she straightened, Hannah realized the woman not only had a baby in the stroller but that she appeared to be pregnant again, as well. "I was enjoying your baby's laughter. I just found out I'm expecting."

"So am I. Congratulations." The woman nodded at her own stomach. "My husband couldn't be here for his daughter's birth, but we're hoping he'll be home for this one."

Hannah's mind was working on the first part of that statement, when the young mother explained. "He was deployed to Iraq. I found out I was pregnant with her—" she reached into the carriage to stroke the child's head "—right after he left."

"I'm glad he'll be here for the new baby."

The woman laughed again. "Me, too. I didn't get to yell any profanities at him during labor."

Hannah smiled. "Who was with you?"

"My mom. Cussing your mother out isn't quite the same." She shook her head. "And, no, I didn't."

"I didn't think you did." Hannah didn't want to think about the fact that her own baby's father probably wouldn't be there for the delivery either. Definitely wouldn't be if it was the donor's child, but even if it was Greg's, she couldn't see him wanting to be there for such an intimate event. The more businesslike they kept things the better for both of them. Something in her chest started aching all over again at the thought.

She'd chosen this route, and she would not allow herself to regret it now. And, honestly, she didn't. Not knowing the father's identity made life a little bizarre at times but she wouldn't go back and undo the pregnancy, even if it was a result of that night.

"I hope your pregnancy goes well," the woman said.

"Thank you. I hope yours does, too."

The baby in the carriage started to fuss, tiny

mewling cries replacing the happy laughter from a few moments earlier. "Sorry," she said. "I have to get moving or she's going to let loose. I just came in to pick up some diapers, but couldn't resist looking around for a while. Unfortunately, big sister is getting hungry."

"I understand completely. I'll let you get back to it."

As the woman moved away from her, the sound of soft singing again floated through the air as the young mother tried to hush the child's cries. A wave of longing went through Hannah. That's what she wanted for her newborn. Not the baby daddy drama she was currently embroiled in but the simple happy singing of a mother to her child. She touched her stomach as if she could somehow transmit some of the woman's joy to her own child.

She started walking again, whispering, "Hey, baby. Be happy, okay?"

But Hannah neither heard not felt anything within her, except a deep sense of loneliness that grew steadily stronger with each step she took.

CHAPTER TEN

STELLA glanced in Hannah's direction as she spoke to whoever was on the phone and pointed toward the receiver and then toward Hannah. "I'll send her right over."

She hung up. "Greg wants you over at the hospital for some reason. Do you mind?"

"Did he say why?"

Her boss never sent for her, always wanting at least one of them at the clinic to attend to patients. But, then again, since he did a lot of the scheduling, he'd know by looking at his little black book that there was a lull for the next two hours. Her nose crinkled. It was also lunchtime and she'd been hoping to sit and eat in peace, gearing up for the afternoon patients.

"Sorry, he didn't give a reason."

"Okay." She sighed and went to get her purse. Was there an emergency with one of their patients? With Claire Taylor, the woman who'd come in a couple of weeks ago?

Hannah arrived at Alaska Regional in fifteen minutes and made her way to the oncology building at the far end of the hospital campus. Greg was waiting for her just inside the entrance, along with a man in a lab coat—so it wasn't about a patient, unless the man was there on a consult. If that was the case, why did they need her?

"I'd like you to meet Bill Watterson," Greg said. "He's a medical geneticist."

Hannah blinked, her mind whirring in confusion. Why would he be introducing her to a...?

Things clicked into place. She shook hands with the newcomer and murmured a greeting she hoped didn't relay her growing anger. He'd never mentioned meeting with a geneticist today. She gave a tight smile and turned to Greg. "Could I speak to you for a minute?"

Bill Watterson, evidently picking up on the tension between them, excused himself, saying he was going to get a coffee and would be back in a few minutes.

As soon as he was out of earshot, Hannah propped her hands on her hips. "You told him?"

Greg frowned for a second, then his face cleared. "I didn't tell him about the pregnancy, no. I wanted his take on my situation, whether or not my sister's myeloid leukemia could be the familial version. If so, I was looking for some reassurance. I thought you might want to hear what he had to say, as well."

"Oh." All the anger seeped away. "Sorry, I just—" She'd thought he'd gone behind her back, but somehow admitting that now didn't seem like a wise thing to do.

"I'm trying to respect your privacy here, Hannah, but I'd be irresponsible if I let you think your child was free from risk when that might not be the case. I did a little research and familial myeloid leukemia is autosomal dominant."

"Meaning it only takes one parent to pass down the gene?"

"Yes."

A blip of fear appeared on her radar screen. "Did your sister have the familial version?"

"I don't know, that's why I talked to Bill. My grandfather also died of leukemia at a relatively young age, but it was never identified as to type."

"And your parents?"

"Neither have had it, but they're in their late fifties. There's still time for it to appear." Greg touched her hand. "Will you meet with Bill? Talk to him with me?"

What choice did she have? She couldn't just turn her back on something this important, not without educating herself on the possibilities. "Yes."

"I thought we'd talk in one of the exam rooms here at the hospital. I didn't think you'd want Stella and the rest of the staff overhearing."

She appreciated him thinking about that, even if he'd just scared ten years off her life. "Thank you."

Bill stood off to the side, sipping a cup of coffee, and she followed Greg as he went over to him. "I think we're ready."

They went to one of the far exam rooms. There were already three chairs set up, so Greg had been prepared, just in case. They each took a seat.

Greg started the conversation. "I've already told you about my sister's and grandfather's leukemia."

"You wanted to know more about the familial version, right?"

"Yes."

Bill glanced at Hannah, who by now was sitting with her icy hands clasped in her lap, another invisible hand clenched tight around her heart. He gave her a reassuring smile.

He knew. Without anyone having to say a word.

"Familial acute myeloid leukemia is fairly rare.

I'm assuming you've already looked up some information."

"I did, but wanted to hear directly from someone with some expertise in the field, otherwise I'm just guessing."

"Well, if you carry the mutation, it'll be in the CEBPA gene. Was your sister tested for type?"

"I don't know. I was in med school at the time, and things were...tense between me and my parents. They played down the seriousness of her illness—at my sister's request—until it was late in the game."

Greg had talked about his sister being his biggest cheerleader when he'd made his decision to go to med school. Had things been tense with his folks because of that decision?

"I see," said Bill. "We might be able to look up her records and see if her doctors identified anything. Any other cases in your family?"

"Just my maternal grandfather. I don't know of anyone further back, although it's possible."

Bill nodded. "The familial cases I've followed have all had an affected parent, as well. If yours are both healthy, I'd say it's unlikely you carry the defect."

"But you couldn't say for sure."

"No, not without sending a sample of your marrow in for testing."

Hannah spoke up. "That's ridiculous, Greg. Why would you do that? If your parents are healthy, then you probably don't have it. Even if you did, the possibility of passing it on is only…" She glanced at Bill, hoping he'd fill in the blank for her.

"It would be roughly fifty percent."

Hannah's heart stalled. "A fifty percent chance that any child he fathered would contract leukemia?"

"No. Just that they'd carry the gene. I would never recommend prenatal testing unless a definite familial link had been determined. In other words, I'd recommend testing for the affected family first." Bill turned to Greg who'd gone pale.

"If you can get me your sister's records, I'll take a look. I really don't think it's going to go any further than that. If it does, we can have you tested. Familial myeloid follows a pretty set pattern, though. From what you've told me, I'm not seeing any cause for concern here."

Greg stood. "Thanks. I'll make sure you get Bethany's records."

Bethany…such a pretty name. A wave of sorrow washed over her. She hadn't even known

Greg's sister's name. But hearing him say it suddenly made her real. Made Hannah even sadder for Greg's loss. The urge to reach across and squeeze his hand came over her.

She stood as well, in an effort to banish the need. "Yes, thank you for talking to us. I appreciate it."

Bill looked from one to the other and smiled. "You're welcome. And good luck. Call me if you have any further questions. Either of you."

With that, he handed Hannah a business card and excused himself, closing the door with a soft click.

"There, do you feel better now?" she asked.

"Not really, no. I still don't know who the hell the father is. Or if I've unintentionally passed something on to it."

This time she didn't resist the urge. She wrapped her hand around his and squeezed. "Look. I wanted a baby and went to a fertility clinic in order to have one. Yes, not knowing whose child it is has put a spanner in the works, but I still want the baby, regardless. If you're feeling guilty, don't. This child is going to be loved more than you could possibly imagine, no matter who the biological father is. Please believe that."

Greg's fingers tightened around hers. "I know it is. You're going to be a wonderful mother. I just wish I could undo what happened between us. That you could have the child you planned to have."

"I already do. Please believe me."

He released her to brush back a short wisp of hair that had fallen over her forehead, smoothing it back with gentle fingers. "Thank you."

"For what?"

"For being you." He leaned over and kissed her cheek. "I'll let you get back to the office."

The meeting had only lasted a half hour so after phoning the clinic to make sure their two o'clock patient hadn't arrived early, Hannah decided to drive the long way back. She needed some time to think before facing anyone at the office. Tiny snowdrops floated across the windshield and blurred the road in front of her. Perfect for her current state of mind, which was just as hazy and indistinct as the view ahead.

Greg's voice had sounded strange when he'd thanked her for being "her." No more insisting that he was going to do right by the baby. If anything, he seemed to be checking things off some invisible list and with each mark he made he backed a little further away from the situation.

It's what she wanted, right? She'd wanted things between them to go back to being simple and uncomplicated. Hadn't wanted any involvement in her life—in her child's life.

But something inside her heart cramped at the thought.

Why? Greg didn't have time for anything else in his life besides work. He'd proven that time and time again. He wasn't likely to change. Not for her. Not for an accidental pregnancy.

It would still just be her and the baby.

She switched on the windshield wipers, and noted a car about a hundred yards in front of her. As she adjusted her speed to maintain a safe distance, something dark and large loomed out of nowhere, moving directly in front of the other car. The vehicle swerved, missing whatever it was— probably a bull moose after a female—but in trying to stay on the road, the driver over-corrected, sliding sideways into a dangerous skid.

Hannah tapped her brakes, praying for the other driver, even as she saw the vehicle leave the road, its passenger door slamming into a nearby tree before coming to a sickening stop. The moose paused, looked in the direction of the accident and then trotted toward a neighboring field as if it hadn't a care in the world.

Oh, God.

After clicking on her hazard lights, she dug for her cell phone, dialing 911 and reporting the accident. She then edged her car forward, getting as close to the other vehicle as she could. Keeping her eye on the moose, which was still visible, she opened her door and half stumbled down the slight embankment as she made her way to the other car. If the moose really was chasing a female, he could turn aggressive in the blink of an eye. As if taunting her, the creature stopped halfway across the field and turned to glare at the two metal interlopers.

Please stay there. She did not want to have to face down a thousand-pound animal while trying to help the occupants of the other vehicle.

She peered inside the driver's side window and saw a woman leaning against her seat belt, the air bag having done nothing to cushion the sideways force of the crash. A trickle of blood made its way down one side of her mouth and dripped from her chin. Hannah tried to open the door, but it was locked.

A cry from somewhere in the back caught her attention, and her eyes widened as she saw an infant carrier strapped into the backseat. It was facing the rear of the car so she couldn't tell what age the child was, but the baby had to be young. The cries grew louder, cutting through the soft plinking of falling snow, which was coming down faster now.

She heard a car stop and glanced up, hoping it was an emergency vehicle, but there'd been no sirens. Nope, it was just another car like hers. Just then a female voice shouted something out the window that sounded like, "Hey, watch out! He's coming back."

She straightened to look, and the blood thrumming through her head rushed straight to her feet. Because the car wasn't the only thing she saw.

The bull moose hadn't drifted away, like she'd hoped it would, but was now headed their way. Although he wasn't moving particularly fast, Hannah knew that could change at any second. He was still on the other side of the road but it wouldn't take much to rile him up. Not at this time of year.

It was then she saw the other moose—a female. The bull had evidently scented her, as evidenced by the animal's head swaying from side to side, white puffs of mist rising from his nostrils as he exhaled. Maybe this was what he'd been after when the woman's car had cut between him and his goal.

Several things went through her mind at once. The car's windows and doors were locked tight, so she couldn't get in, neither could she get the occupants out. The baby inside the car was crying louder now, his wails turning to piercing shrieks, which could serve to further agitate the moose.

And the most terrifying thing of all was the realization that she was standing directly between the huge bull moose and his prospective mate.

Just as that last thought registered, the moose lowered his head and charged.

CHAPTER ELEVEN

GREG'S head swiveled to the right as a familiar name hit his ears.

Hannah Lassiter. The words *moose, roof* and *unknown injuries* also came through. His blood turned to ice in his veins just as the cell phone at his hip began to vibrate.

He glanced at the readout, noting it was the office. He punched the talk button, but before the person on the other end of the line could get in a simple hello, he barked into the receiver, "Where's Hannah?"

Stella's answer came through the line. "I was calling to let you know she phoned here a few seconds ago. She's at the scene of an accident."

"Is she hurt?"

"I don't think so. But a moose has evidently gone on a rampage, and she's trapped. State troopers are on their way and Dispatch is sending an EMT unit, as well."

"Where?"

"Mountain View Road."

"Mountain View? Are you sure?"

"That's what she said."

"Okay, Stella, thanks. I'm heading up there. Page me if there's an emergency."

He clicked off and raced to the hospital parking lot, where he gunned the engine of his BMW and tore out. He had no idea how far out she was, but he could already hear the wail of a siren, probably heading to the scene. He'd just follow behind them.

Hell, had the meeting with Bill Watterson upset her so much that she'd needed to get away from everything? There was no other reason for her driving up Mountain View Road when Debarr was a straight shot to the clinic. Unless she'd needed to think about things.

He pressed the gas pedal in an effort to catch up to the emergency services vehicle. Not many cars were on the road at the moment, so he wasn't worried about creating a problem. All he wanted to do was reach Hannah and make sure she and the baby were okay…that they'd simply come across an accident and had called for help.

Five minutes later, he saw he was wrong. Hannah was perched on top of the roof of a small SUV while a bull moose—as big or bigger than the vehicle itself—stood a few feet away. The black car had a big dent in the driver's side door, whether from the accident or from being charged by the moose, he had no idea.

Even as he thought it, the animal snorted then lowered its head and pushed against the vehicle with its enormous spread of antlers. The wheels on that side of the car left the ground, sending Hannah scrambling for a handhold on the roof racks. The vehicle came crashing back down as the pressure was suddenly released.

Damn.

The EMT guys got out of their vehicle but remained behind the open doors, not daring to make a move toward the enraged animal.

His heart in his throat, he knew if the moose somehow flipped that vehicle, Hannah could be crushed in the process. Or if she wasn't, moose had been known to stomp people into the ground, killing them. Even as he thought it, the moose repeated the act and the vehicle tipped higher than it had the last time.

Without thinking about the consequences, Greg opened the door to his car and got out, rounding the hood as he yelled. "Hey! Over here! Come this way!"

The moose's head came up and the car dropped back into place so fast that Hannah was thrown sideways, her legs coming over the edge right in the space between the moose's antlers. If the animal's glance swung back that way...

Even as he thought it, Hannah kicked, scrambling back onto the roof and hunkering down low. She was from Idaho, from what he understood, but he had no idea how much experience she had with large game.

Moose could be unpredictable, appearing calm one second and then striking out with shocking speed the next. He'd heard of instances where tourists had tried to approach a resting moose, not realizing the calm demeanor could change in the space of a heartbeat. Tragedy had happened on more than one occasion.

Greg took another step, anger rising up fast and quick in his gut. Where the hell were the state troopers? He yelled again, waving his arms to keep the animal focused on him. Maybe it would abandon Hannah and come after him instead. The moose swung around in a ninety-degree arc, one of its massive antlers scraping along the length of the SUV as it did. Hannah looked at him, her frown apparent even from this distance. She shook her head, silently trying to warn him off.

The EMT guys had ventured a little farther from their truck, probably wondering what the crazy cancer doctor thought he was doing.

Just then Greg heard the sound of twin sirens and before he had time to think, two state troopers squealed off the road and in front of his car.

The noise and growing number of bodies was evidently too much for the moose to handle, and he gave one last snort, before whirling and trotting away from the vehicles. Greg waited a second or two to make sure he wasn't coming back, then hurried around the police cars, shouting that he was a doctor when they acted like they might stop him. He met the EMT guys at the stricken SUV and reached up toward Hannah. She let him wrap his hands around her waist and pluck her from the roof.

"You okay?"

She leaned against him for a moment, her body trembling in reaction. "Fine, but we need to get inside the car. There's an injured woman."

One of the EMTs tried the doorhandle then called for everyone to stand back. Greg, his arm around her waist, edged Hannah back and to the side so that she was facing away from the vehicle. The paramedic broke the window with a metal instrument and then reached in to click the automatic door locks. The child in the back, who'd finally stopped crying, started up again at the sound of the glass shattering.

Hannah pulled away and went to the back door, opening it. She quickly checked the child for injuries while he was still strapped into the seat. Her heart wrenched when the child's arms went up in an age-old request to be picked up, "Just a second, sweetheart. I'll get you."

"We've got a broken left clavicle and possible rib fractures up here. Get the back brace." The EMT met her eyes from across the seats. She recognized him from the hospital, and he evidently recognized her as well, because he didn't even question her qualifications. "What have you got back there?"

"I'm not seeing any obvious injuries, the car seat did its job. I think he's just scared."

"Great. We'll transport him anyway, just to be safe."

Hannah unclicked the car seat and gingerly lifted the child from it, ducking down to bring him out of the damaged vehicle. She propped him against her shoulder, rubbing his back through his thick layers of clothing and murmuring softly to him.

The whole world seemed to fade away as she held him, a sense of magic and mystery flowing from his small frame to hers. His crying stopped almost immediately. She turned to Greg with a smile she couldn't contain.

He came forward a step. "He's okay, then?"

"I think he's perfect."

Some dark, powerful force flashed through his gaze as he eyed the pair of them, one side of his mouth finally curving up in a half smile. He started to reach toward her, then his smile faded and he averted his eyes. Without a word he moved away to check on the woman's condition, although the EMTs looked to have everything well in hand.

The two troopers came over and asked for a quick rundown of events, which Hannah relayed to the best of her ability, although she was still shaking both inside and out. One of the officers jotted everything down on a clipboard and then turned it, asking her to sign the statement. She couldn't. Not while holding the baby. "Hold on for a second."

She hurried over to Greg and held the infant toward him. "Can you take him for a minute? I need to sign something for the police."

He looked like he might refuse, but finally took the child from her, holding him awkwardly under the arms. The poor thing's legs dangled straight down, a bemused expression coming over his tiny face.

"No, like this," she instructed, helping him slide an arm under the baby's legs while guiding his other hand to the baby's chest to stabilize him in a kind of modified swing position. Greg seemed stiff and uncomfortable, but something in her chest melted at how he looked holding the baby. He looked…

Like a father.

Biting her lip, she swung away before he saw anything in her eyes. Going back over to the officers, she signed the paperwork. "Let me know if you need anything else."

"We will. Thank you, ma'am. We'll call for a tow truck for the vehicle. Do you have a ride home?"

"Yes, I have my car." She motioned to the emergency lane of the highway, where her car was still sitting, emergency flashers engaged.

As the officers each got into their respective vehicles, filling out papers and talking on their radios, she wrapped her arms around her waist, realizing how very cold she was all of a sudden.

She'd leaped out of her car without her coat when she'd seen the accident, her thin turtleneck and camisole the only coverings she'd had on. Everything was damp, including her hair.

The snow had stopped falling at least, but the temperature felt like it was still dropping, or was that because she'd been trapped on top of a freezing car for the past half hour?

Something warm and familiar settled across her shoulders, his scent filling her senses. Greg. But where was…?

"The baby?" she asked.

"The EMTs are loading him and his mom into the truck. They're both going to be fine."

Another hard shiver went through her as more of the cold air made it through her sweater to her skin. A soft curse ruffled her hair. "You're half-frozen. Where's your jacket, Hannah?"

She had to think for a second. "The accident happened so fast, and I wanted to make sure everyone was okay. There was no time to grab it from my car. Then the moose came back…there was no time to do anything but get on top of the SUV."

"Come on, let's get you someplace warm."

Pulling her away from the gathering crowd of onlookers, he helped her into his vehicle and reached over to switch it on. The still-warm engine sent heated air swirling around the interior and Greg got in the other side, holding her icy hands in his own. Between the car's heater vents and the body next to her, warmth slowly penetrated her frozen core.

"Better?" he asked.

"Mmm…" she murmured, leaning closer with another shiver. "Your hands are so warm."

He shifted to put an arm around her and pulled her toward him. Hannah had no idea how his body could generate so much heat, especially as he was coatless and hatless as well. All she knew was that if she could wriggle her way beneath his skin right now, she would.

They sat there for what seemed like forever then he broke the silence. "Give me your car keys."

She sighed, not moving, as the heat continued to work its magic. "They're in the car, along with my purse." She needed to go, but couldn't work up the energy to prise herself from Greg's body or from the interior of the car.

"Wait here. I'll be right back."

She cringed when he pulled away, depriving her of his warmth. The sensation was even worse when he opened the car door and slid out. Then he shut it again and Hannah leaned back in her seat, letting her eyes close. The combination of the meeting with the geneticist and the adrenaline from the moose attack did what several sleepless nights had been unable to accomplish: send a wave of exhaustion over her. She yawned and let her body go utterly limp.

Just a second or two, that's all she needed. Then she'd be able to drum up enough energy to drive back to the clinic and see to the rest of their patients. She tried to remember whose names she'd seen on the schedule that morning, but there was nothing inside her head but a big black hole. It was as if she'd been drained of everything. Her hands went to her stomach, rubbing it softly as she gave way to the tiredness seeping through her.

Vaguely, she was aware that Greg had returned and that his car was now in motion, but no power under heaven could have wrenched her eyelids apart. Instead, she sat there, her head lolling back and forth on the seat as the vehicle made gentle turns for the next several minutes before stopping.

The clinic. They must have arrived. Time to wake up.

But her muscles felt as floppy as a piece of lettuce that had been frozen and then defrosted. The car pulled forward again for a few seconds, then the purr of the engine cut off. A door opened and closed, but this time no icy gusts of wind blew across her cheeks, just slightly heated air.

Her eyelids finally obeyed her commands to open, her brain struggling to make sense of what she was seeing. They were inside some kind of white enclosure. The clinic didn't have a parking garage.

Didn't matter. Maybe Greg would just let her sit here and sleep a while longer. Then her door opened.

No such luck, evidently.

However, instead of nudging her to get her to move, her seat belt unclicked—when had she buckled it?—and something soft and fluffy enveloped her before she was lifted from the car.

Lifted?

Oh, but the girls at the office were going to have a field day if Greg carried her into the clinic. She tried to protest, shifting in his arms, only to have a soft voice shush her, tell her it was okay to sleep for a while.

It was?

Well, she wasn't going to argue with him. Besides, her lids were already sliding shut again.

A minute later something soft met her back, her shoes came off, and the fluffy object from the car was tucked around her. She could have sworn warm lips pressed against her forehead for a long second but that must be part of the wonderful dream she was having. Whatever it was, she was willing to sink deep into it for a few minutes.

Then she'd rouse herself back to the real world and all of its worries.

Right now there was just her and Greg and this decadent sensation of...of... She struggled to put her finger on it, before settling on the only word that came to mind: *peace.*

Greg's patients were at the clinic, and he was at home. Something unheard of.

But from the moment he'd felt the sheer iciness of Hannah's hands, he'd known what he was going to do. He asked one of the police officers to see to it that her car made it to his house. The officer had glanced toward Greg's car, where Hannah was half-asleep, and nodded. Then Greg retrieved her handbag and called Stella, giving her an abbreviated version of the story.

"Poor thing," the other woman said. "We can cover for you this afternoon. There are only three patients left. Take her home and let her get some sleep."

Greg was pretty sure Stella was referring to Hannah's home and not his own, but somehow that was where they wound up.

He didn't dare stretch out beside her on his bed, and there were no guest bedrooms in his house. His hours precluded having any overnight visitors—female or otherwise. His parents had never asked to stay with him, opting for a nearby hotel room on the one occasion they'd come from Ketchikan to visit.

One visit in ten years.

Damn. He hadn't been a very good son since his sister had died. It was easy to blame it on the distance between Anchorage and Ketchikan, but how hard was it to pick up a telephone and give them a call? Then again, his father had held a grudge for a very long time after Greg had turned down his offer—maybe he still did. It was something they'd never talked through and resolved. And his mother had been unwilling to take sides. Bethany had been the only one who could see through to Greg's heart. And now she was gone.

Shaking away those troubling thoughts, he moved back to the situation at hand. What was he going to do about Hannah? He'd allowed her to eat into his office hours in a way he'd never let anyone else do, not even his parents.

It was because of her pregnancy. It had to be.

You don't even know if the child is yours, Greg.

When does it stop? When you have a patient go into crisis and die because you aren't there for them—just like Bethany's doctor had done?

No. He'd vowed to be different. To be someone his patients could call day or night. Just like he'd urged Claire Taylor to do.

He remembered Hannah's comment about seeing him rush past the chemo room from time to time. Yes, he'd begun peeking in there in recent weeks and greeting his patients when he saw them, but what about before? What about when it had been Hannah sitting in one of those chairs?

He'd been oblivious, just like he'd accused his sister's doctor of being.

Hell. His thoughts jumped from one thing to the other, but that assurance that he was doing the right thing was no longer in the spot it used to be.

The situation with Hannah had messed with his head, and he wasn't sure he was ever going to be able to go back to who he was before. Neither was he sure he wanted to.

So what did he want?

He glanced toward the dark hallway leading to his bedroom.

He wanted something he couldn't possibly have. But that didn't stop him from wanting it just the same.

CHAPTER TWELVE

THE smell of bacon roused her from a blissful dream. One where Greg held their child in his arms and slid beside her on the bed, leaning over to kiss her forehead.

She smiled up at him as she drew her fingers across his cheek and murmured that she loved him even more than…

Bacon?

Her eyes flew open. Yes, she'd just told a man she loved him more than a strip of nitrite-loaded meat. Okay, so it had been in her dream, not in real life.

And she didn't love him…not more than bacon, not less than bacon. Not at all.

She blinked as the room came into focus. Wait. This wasn't her bedroom. The beige microfiber blanket wasn't hers either. She remembered the moose ramming the car, the injured woman inside, the cold and this very blanket being carefully folded around her as she'd been lifted from the car.

Lifted from the car…

Oh, no! She hadn't gone back to work. And what about their patients?

Had Greg returned to the clinic and finished the workday without her?

Great. He now thought she was less than useless. It had to be all the messed-up hormones that went along with a pregnancy. She was just going to have to push through them. She couldn't just curl up on a cot at the office whenever the urge hit her.

Turning her head, she looked at the pillow on the other side of the bed. It was still flat across the top. No indentation from a head, and the bedspread hadn't been pulled back. Greg hadn't slept here at all.

Maybe it was still today. No, wait, yesterday. She glanced at the clock. Seven…squinting, she noted there was no red glowing dot beside the p.m. symbol, which meant it was morning.

So she'd slept here all night.

And the scent of bacon meant Greg was still at home. He was normally in the office by now, catching up on paperwork.

Except it was Saturday. At least she thought it was. She did the math in her head. Yes, Saturday. She assumed Greg didn't normally work weekends, although she wouldn't put anything past the man. He'd certainly gone in that Saturday when Claire had called.

A soft knock sounded at the door, and she realized he'd closed it at some point. "Come in."

The door opened and her boss appeared in the entrance, his hair damp, a plaid flannel shirt rolled up his forearms. She hadn't taken him for a flannel kind of guy, but she kind of liked the rugged air it gave him.

"How are you feeling?"

She cleared her throat before answering. "Guilty."

His brows went up. "Why?"

"Um, I was supposed to be working yesterday, and instead I conked out in your car on the way back. Sorry about that. Did you have to see to the rest of the patients on your own?"

There was a short pause before he responded. "Stella took care of it."

"Took care of..." Another wave of guilt washed over her. "You didn't go back either?"

He took a step inside the room. "There was nothing urgent. I'll go in for a few hours later today."

So he did work on weekends. She vaguely remembered him coming into her hospital room the day after her surgery. That had been a Saturday, as well. At least, she thought it was. Her memories of those days were a little suspect as she'd been an emotional wreck.

He had to work, and here she was lounging in his house. No wonder he was trying to wake her up. "Sorry. I'll get dress—" Okay, so she'd never gotten *un*dressed. And exactly how was she supposed to get home? "Where's my car?"

"It's in the driveway."

That was strange. She remembered him asking about her keys but just, like her surgery, those memories were cloaked in a foggy haze that she couldn't quite penetrate. "How did it get here?"

"One of the police officers said he'd see to it. He put the keys through the mailbox slot on the front door."

She sat up. "Have you heard anything about the woman and her baby?"

He smiled and leaned against the doorpost. "You mean the ones currently in my bed or the ones from yesterday?"

Yesterday. So she had slept all afternoon and all night. In Greg's bed, of all things. "Yesterday."

"I checked this morning. Mom has a slight concussion, broken collarbone and some bruised ribs.

The baby is with his father, who flew back from a business trip to be with them."

Hannah's heart tightened. What if something similar happened to her? There would be no husband to come running. Where would her baby go?

Her parents would fly in and take care of the child.

Why did that thought bring her no comfort? "So she's going to be okay."

"Yes. They'll probably keep her for observation one more day then they'll release her."

"I'm glad she's okay."

Greg moved the rest of the way into the room and sat on the edge of the bed, smoothing a few strands of hair back from her temples. "As for you, let's try not to bait any more moose traps in the near future, okay?"

"Believe me, if I'd known that big guy was going to come at me, I'd have had second thoughts about getting out of my car."

"Sure you would."

Okay, so he had her there. She hadn't known how badly hurt the other car's occupants had been. There's no way she'd have waited around for the moose to decide the vehicle wasn't worth its trouble. But she also wouldn't have purposely gone running across its path either. "I wasn't trying to get myself killed."

"That's good." There was a pause. "I wouldn't want to have to replace you."

His eyes held hers, and she tried to decipher the changing emotions she saw in them, but failed. All she knew was that he wasn't angry, and that fact made her relax. "Admit it. You kind of like having me around." When his eyes darkened to black, she realized how that had sounded and quickly added, "At the clinic, I mean."

He didn't respond for a second or two then his hand withdrew. "Of course."

A sudden awkward silence fell between them, which she tried to break with the first thing she could think of. "Is that bacon I smell?"

"It is. I've also whipped up an omelet. Interested in sharing?"

The words brought back memories of another time they'd shared food. At the clinic. She'd fallen asleep there as well, and disastrous things had happened afterward. Better not to keep sitting here, especially not after the dream she'd had before he'd knocked on the door. "Definitely, if there's enough."

He stood and held out a hand. "There's plenty."

She let him help her out of bed, the tangle of blankets causing her to career forward when she tried to get her feet underneath herself. He caught her, a hand at her back holding her against him for a second or two before releasing her again and taking a step back.

"I, ah, need to use your restroom first, if that's okay," she said.

"It's right through there." He nodded at a door on the other side of the bedroom. "I'll get the plates ready, so come out when you're ready. Do you take butter or jam on your toast?"

"Both?" Bad for her, she knew, but something about the taste of warm melty butter mixed with fruit was one she hadn't been able to give up.

"Both it is. I'll see you in a few minutes."

Hannah went into the restroom and put her hands on the sink as she stared into the mirror. She must have slept like a rock, because her hair wasn't sticking up at all angles like it normally did. She'd be glad when it grew out enough to rake back into a ponytail or put up in a clip. For now, she settled with dragging her fingers through it and coaxing it to settle into place. She found a tube of toothpaste in a cup and squirted a dab on her finger, scrubbing her teeth as best she could. She wasn't about to ask if he had a spare toothbrush in a package somewhere. Not because she wouldn't love to clean her teeth but because she didn't want to think of him keeping spare toothbrushes on hand for occasional overnight guests—of the female variety.

She had to admit she didn't hear a whole lot of rumors about her boss being paired up with women at the hospital, and she knew he wasn't involved with anyone at the clinic as everyone there was either married or spoken for. But that didn't mean he didn't meet people somewhere else.

When would he even have the time, though, with a schedule like his?

Sighing, she finished washing up the best she could before following her nose. She found Greg sliding the second half of a fluffy-looking omelet onto a plate. "I thought you said you didn't cook."

He glanced up, his eyes going over her from head to toe. "You're seeing my entire repertoire. I don't normally eat anything but breakfast at home."

"What do you eat when you're off duty?"

"I manage."

That sounded suspiciously like wolfing down takeout food night after night.

He set a plastic disposable plate in front of her across the small bar. Strange. Did he not have a set of real dishes? The sink was empty as well—and there was no sign of a dishwasher—so they weren't all dirty.

Now that she had a moment to look around, she saw that the great room was as sparsely furnished as the bedroom had been. A couch and an easy chair sat across from a large-screen television, which was hung on a wall, but there were no coffee tables or end tables. There was a beige washcloth resting on the hardwood floor beside the recliner, which she could imagine him resting drinks on.

A state-of-the-art treadmill was pushed against the far wall, a handtowel slung over its digital panel. The machine's incline was set to a painful-looking angle, but that was it—no other furniture except the two barstools they were currently using.

And other than the floor, there were no flat sur-faces to set pictures or knick-knacks on. "Did you just move in or something?"

He sat across from her at the bar. "No, I've lived here for about five years, why?"

"It's just…empty."

Five years. And he had nothing to show for it.

Greg's glance trailed around the room before he shrugged. "I'm not here that much."

If she'd had any doubts about him pushing himself to the point of neglect, he'd set them to rest. Her own house was filled with things that made her happy—baskets of soft quilts and afghans beside a comfortable couch. Just right for settling in with a book or a chick flick. Some of her grandmother's things were sprinkled here and there, and an old Victorian rocking chair sat in a place of honor in her living room.

Her front room drew her in the moment she hit that front door and helped her relax. The first thing she did was kick off her shoes in the entryway—symbolic of leaving her workday behind her—and pad across the deep-pile carpet on the floor.

She didn't have time for a pet other than three fish in a large terracotta pot on the back patio. The constant sound of trickling water from the submersible pump was soothing, as were the goldfish—rescued from the kill tank at a local pet store—who came up to greet her, their mouths opening and closing to an internal beat. She liked to imagine them dancing and singing, moving to the tune of the falling water. She'd gotten her little guys soon after her treatments had finished and they'd grown and flourished. Just like her.

Greg's sterile environment, on the other hand,

made her feel lonely, somehow, even though it wasn't her house.

"Hannah? Are you okay?"

Greg's voice interrupted her thoughts, and she realized she'd been staring off into space—or, worse, staring at him. "I'm fine. Just feeling slightly out of it still."

"You had quite a day yesterday." He forked a bite of omelet into his mouth, and she glanced down at her own plate. Eggs filled with what looked like a creamy mixture of broccoli and cheese, expertly folded and cut in half. Toast with…yep, butter *and* grape jelly, and four neat slices of bacon.

"Wow, I never eat this much in the morning."

"It's probably time you started to."

She blinked for a second then realized he was talking about her pregnancy. "I guess you're right. It's not all about me anymore."

Greg's fork faltered on its way back to his mouth, and he set it on his plate. "I guess it's not," he murmured.

Something about the way he said it made another wave of loneliness hit her. Not for herself this time but for him. "Sometimes it's good to be reminded of that."

If he understood what she was getting at, he ignored it, steering the conversation in another direction instead. "I forgot to ask. Do you want to put a call in to your doctor and have her check you over after what happened yesterday?"

"It's Saturday."

"So?"

"I feel fine. Besides, I'm sure she has a life outside work." As soon as she'd said it, she realized he really *didn't* see what the big deal was. Did he assume that all doctors kept the kinds of hours that he did? Surely he knew better.

"It's her job."

"Are you serious?" She took a bite of her omelet to stifle the flow of words that wanted to pour out of her mouth.

"She's an obstetrician. I'm sure she's used to working crazy hours. Babies can't be programmed to arrive during a nine-to-five workday." The words came out with a bitter edge she didn't understand.

She swallowed her food. "Exactly. Which is why I don't want to call her for any little thing."

"You were attacked by a moose—banged around by him. Isn't it better to be safe than sorry?"

"I'm fine. Not even bruised. I think my recovery consisted of sleeping." She set her jaw. "I'm not calling her."

"Fine." A flash of anger went through his eyes, but he didn't say anything more.

There was no sound for the next few minutes, other than eating. Hannah kept her head down, wishing her hair was long enough to shade her face and afford her a bit more privacy.

"I'm sorry. You're right." Greg's soft voice came across the bar, and she looked up in surprise as he continued. "I forget that other doctors don't get the kind of satisfaction from their jobs that I do."

"Just because they don't work themselves into the ground it doesn't mean they don't find satisfaction in what they do. I enjoy having weekends off. It helps me recharge my batteries."

"I'm not judging you or anyone else. It's simply how I've chosen to live my life."

How he'd chosen to live his life. So he'd made a conscious decision at some point in time to work this hard? If so, she thought she knew when that had been.

"Because of your sister?"

His fork stopped halfway to his mouth. "What do you mean?"

"You said you became an oncologist because of

her." She forced the words past the lump in her throat. "Is that why you work so hard?"

"Yes." The word came out as simply and smoothly as silk. Things clicked into place a little bit further.

"You once said it was because you wanted to help others like her, but is it more than that? Do feel guilty for being alive? Are you paying some type of penance?"

He seemed to consider that for a minute. "No, but we were pretty close. Her death came as a shock—it was more sudden than anyone expected, a couple of days after one of her chemo treatments. Her doctor was nowhere to be found when she got to the hospital. I never want that to happen with my patients."

"You can't be available every second of every day."

"No, but I also don't have to live at the golf course or the ski slopes, depending on the season."

"Are you saying that's what your sister's doctor did?"

"He has quite a reputation in Ketchikan, from what I've learned."

"That's terrible. I'm so sorry."

His left shoulder lifted and fell. "It was a long time ago. I'm over it."

Was he? His behavior said he wasn't.

"It never seems that long ago." She spoke from the experience of her own health crisis. Maybe someday in the distant future she'd look back at her cancer as some tiny speck in her rearview mirror instead of the huge black mass that stood just off to the side, waiting to slide into her path and derail her dreams. Just like that moose from yesterday had sent the other car careening off the road. It could happen suddenly. Without warning.

Even as she thought it, the fear inched closer, rising in front of her.

You're fine, Hannah. Healthy. Strong.

She pulled in a deep cleansing breath, let it back out. Sucked down another.

A hand covered hers. "Hey, I'm sorry. I keep forgetting you've been down that path, too."

"It's stupid. I just can't seem to get past it, to…" Horror of horror, tears washed up her throat and gathered in her eyes. She blinked furiously, trying to suppress them in any way she could.

Greg got up from his seat and came around to the other side of the bar, wrapping his arms around her shoulders and pressing her face into the solid warmth of his chest. "I know the feeling. I promise you, I do. If I could do something to make sure the cancer doesn't ever come back, I would. I swear it."

"I know." She sniffed. "It's not you. It's me. And I know you'd do the same for your sister, if you could. You're trying to make it up to her with each patient you save."

He cupped her face, tilting it so she was forced to look at him. His thumbs stroked across her cheekbones sending a slow shiver through her that had nothing to do with the cold. Nothing to do with fear. "You're probably one of the few people who could ever understand that. One of the few who could fathom why I never wanted children…a wife."

A stabbing pain went through her chest, and she tried to pull away, only to have him hold her in place. She'd known this all along, was a fool to believe him when he'd said he wanted to be involved with this child, if it was his.

He didn't want a baby. Any baby.

"Let me go, Greg, please." Otherwise the tears she'd successfully fought back could start gushing through the crack in her soul.

"I can't." His eyes bored into hers. "I didn't want kids, but the thought that this—" one hand left her face to splay low across her tummy "—might be mine has messed with my head in ways you can't even imagine."

Maybe that kiss on her forehead yesterday hadn't been her imagination after all. Maybe he was just as confused as she seemed to be. She'd gone from wanting to stay as far away from him as she could to wanting to be closer to him than any human being possibly could. If nothing else, she could admit it.

"Mine, too." She forced a smile. "It was a whole lot easier when I thought those cells came from the end of a catheter."

"Easier." He smiled back at her. "But not quite as much fun."

Any remaining tears receded at his gentle, teasing tone. "You know what they say about natural being better than modified. We could always put a stamp on you and call you organic."

He laughed, then his head dipped, his cheek sliding against hers. The still rough whiskers from last night scraped across her skin, and his scent filled her nostrils. Then his lips were at her ear, causing gooseflesh to rise on her arms as he whispered into it, "I think what's going on between us is pretty organic."

His words sent a jet of raw need spurting through her system, sweeping along her senses until every cell in her body was waiting in hungry anticipation.

Those cells didn't have long to wait because he soon retraced the same path his cheek had taken, only this time with his mouth. When he reached her lips he hovered there for a second or two as if debating options.

Only there was no option, even he had to see that. "Kiss me, Greg."

Very slowly, his hand moved to her nape, fingers sliding into the short strands of her hair. "I don't want to do this."

Oh, yes, he did. She could feel it in the tension radiating from him, in the way his hand applied just enough pressure to keep her from moving away from him. And Hannah gloried in it. Rejoiced that a man—*this* man—could be so attracted to her that he was willing to ignore his rational side just to have her. And he wanted her in spite of the effects of the chemotherapy that were still very evident in her body and mind—her short hair, her scars, her moments of unbridled terror.

He didn't seem to care about any of that.

And hanging in the balance was everything he

claimed to want in life—everything he said he *didn't* want.

That didn't stop his head from beginning that fatal descent, didn't stop his lips from meeting hers in a delirious, electrifying kiss from which there was no hope of escape.

And the last thing Hannah wanted was to escape.

All she wanted, was him.

CHAPTER THIRTEEN

FIVE seconds after Hannah wrapped her arms around his neck, strong hands swept her off the barstool and carried her somewhere. She didn't open her eyes to look. Didn't care where they were going.

All she knew was that there was nothing like the sensation of this man's lips on hers, the crazy things his touch did to her on the inside—and on the outside, where her nipples were already pressing against her shirt, her body moistening in anticipation of what was going to happen.

What she *hoped* was going to happen.

Greg moved her in a way that no other man ever had. From the moment he'd come onto the scene, her life had gone topsy-turvy. In some ways those changes had been terrible beyond belief, and in other ways they had been more wonderful than words could express.

This was one such moment.

He kicked at a door, muttering a curse under his

breath when it evidently bounced back and caught him in the shoulder. She smiled against his lips. "Oh, an ouchie. Do you want me to kiss it?"

"No." The growled word was followed by a quick hard press of his mouth to hers. "I have better places for you to kiss."

A wave of need rose up inside her, and just like the time in his office she wanted him to consume her in a fiery rush, wanted him so badly that she shook with it. It made her crazy, confused her in ways that she'd never been before.

She loved it. And hated it.

And where she should grab on to the latter thought and start waving it like a white flag in front of her raging libido, her mind embraced the former, to the point where she didn't know if the idea of love referred to the man himself or what he did to her.

Please don't let it be the man.

The plea had barely been processed when her back met the same soft surface it had yesterday afternoon, only this time Greg followed her down. And his reassuring kiss was not on her forehead but had moved to her throat where the touch was anything but comforting. Instead it made her squirm against him, arching her neck to give him better access.

"I thought you had places you wanted *me* to kiss."

"I lied." One of his jeans-clad legs nudged between her thighs, the weight of it resting on her most sensitive spot. She resisted the urge to shift her hips to increase the pressure.

His mouth slid down to her collarbone, licking across something before kissing it gently.

The scar from her port.

The almost reverent act made her breath catch and tears once again appeared on the horizon, but he'd already moved lower, to where the V of her shirt dipped, showing the slightest curve of her breast.

His lifted his head, all teasing gone. "Do you want me to use protection?"

Her mind whirred. She was already pregnant, had already had him without anything between them. It seemed silly to backtrack at this late point. "No."

Greg moved back up and took her mouth again, showing her with his tongue and teeth that he approved of her decision. Her own heart threatened to hammer its way from her chest as he mimicked the long strokes from a few weeks ago. She reached up to hold him against her, needing him to continue doing exactly what he was doing.

He didn't disappoint, sliding his left hand to her breast, finding her nipple even through the padding of her bra. Sensation arced from her breast to her center, where his leg was still exerting delicious pressure.

Moaning against his mouth, she couldn't stop herself from lifting her hips this time, and a wave of need hit her system when she did, moving through her like wildfire. She pressed closer still.

Greg reacted by shifting his weight and removing temptation.

"No! What are you doing?"

He kissed her mouth before answering. "Slowing things down a little bit. Last time was—" he paused "—great, but I want this to last."

Last? Who cared about lasting? She wanted him, and she wanted him now.

But Greg evidently had no intention of letting her call the shots because despite her low sound of displeasure he smoothed her hair off her forehead then kissed her eyes, her cheeks, the tip of her chin.

When he acted like he was going to avoid her mouth, she put her hands to the back of his head and pulled him to her. He obliged, his lips sliding across hers repeatedly, the subtle friction nearly driving her insane before he finally kissed her the way she wanted to be kissed.

She melted with a sigh.

"Better?" he whispered.

"Much."

Her neck, which had been straining up in an effort to reach him, relaxed into the pillows with a sigh as he deepened the kiss, following her down. Her hands, no longer needing their feverish grip on his head, wandered over his back, feeling the bunching of muscles as he moved in time with the give and take of their joined mouths.

The same way those muscles would react when they were joined in other areas. Would he have to get rid of the bed afterward, like he'd done with his desk?

She almost laughed. These little rendezvous could end up costing him a fortune if this became a regular event.

No. Don't think about that right now. Just enjoy the time you have together. That's what you vowed to do, right? Take life as it came and not worry about what might happen in the future.

Yes. That was better.

So much better that…

Her hands went from holding on to shoving at his chest.

His "What are you—?" was drowned by her laughter as she turned the tables, flipping him onto his back in a smooth move that would have made any ju jitsu instructor proud.

"I assume you had a reason for doing that?" His brows went up.

"Mmm-hmm." She wiggled her hips against his rigid length. "I'm taking charge."

He groaned. "I thought we'd already settled this. We're going slow."

"I'm not interested in slow." To prove her point, she sat up, her legs straddling his hips—where she could still feel a definite spark of interest— and stripped off her shirt. Her bra followed a second later. She trailed the garment across his lips, up one of his arms. He wrapped his hand around it and flung it to the side.

"Hannah…"

"Spoilsport." She leaned forward, her breasts flattening against his chest, and used her hand to cover his mouth. "I've already decided how this is going to go, so no use trying to stop me."

He nipped at her hand until she removed it. "Believe me, I have no intention of stopping you."

"Well, good." She sat up again. "Then you won't mind if I do this."

She slid higher, until she was on his belly, her hand reaching behind her to find the zipper of his jeans and that delicious hard ridge that lay just beneath it. Placing her palm over the swell of his flesh, she stroked him for a second or two, until he sat up in a rush, dumping her back onto his lap.

"My turn," he said, his breathing not quite steady.

His hands slid over the skin of her back, hot and urgent as they headed down, edging beneath the waistband of her slacks and cupping her bare butt.

She smiled. "Oh, I like that."

"Yes? Then how about this?" He jerked her forward until she was pressed tight against him, his strong grip rocking her along his length. The breath she'd been holding rushed from her lungs in an audible gasp as a sudden jolt of sensation gripped her center. From zero to a hundred in under a second and a half.

Her eyes closed at the heady knowledge that he was using her body to massage his own, to heighten his pleasure, even as hers skyrocketed, as well. Her thighs, forced wide by his hips, made her fully aware that only a few centimeters of clothing separated them, and even that couldn't stop the torturous friction that had her rushing closer to oblivion with each passing second.

She gripped his shoulders for all she was worth as he increased the speed and pressure, his own body static, while hers rose and fell. Her teeth dug into her lower lip, knowing if she was going to ask him to slow down, it needed to be now. But she'd started this…claimed she didn't want to go slow… so he was giving her exactly what she'd demanded. What she wanted. What she…

The black depths of his pupils appeared before her as she struggled in vain to stay afloat, but this wave was too tall, too wild, too…

She buried her face against his neck with a hoarse cry as everything inside of her seemed to implode all at once, her mind blanking out as her body shattered into a thousand pieces and then fell back together again in a rush.

Hannah was vaguely aware that while Greg's hands still held her tightly against him, he was no longer dragging her along at a punishing pace. But his body was still hard. Still tense.

She leaned back to look at him, trying to breathe

as she gathered her thoughts. "Wh-what, exactly, was that supposed to be?"

His crooked grin was unrepentant. "That was fast. Just like you wanted."

Fast.

It had been that. And more. Her legs were still trembling from the force of her explosion.

"What about you?"

"Me?" His hands came up, one splaying across the middle of her back and the other cupping her head. "I already told you. I'm all about slow."

As if to demonstrate exactly what he meant, he laid her gently backward an inch at a time, until she was again lying on the bed, her head at the opposite end this time. Once she was there, he reached down and unbuttoned her jeans, the act taking her all the way back to the first step on the stairway she'd just climbed. She looked at the distance from here to where she'd just been and sighed.

Mmm.

Slow sounded like a very, very good idea.

"Annie, look what someone made for you." Greg brought out a neon purple hat one of his other patients—who'd seen Annie in his office a week ago—had knitted for her out of some kind of soft furry yarn.

The child's eyes widened as she reached for it, her fingers sinking deep as she hugged it to her. Her happiness contrasted with the bittersweet emotions circling within his own chest.

"It's so soft," she said. "Just like my kitty's fur. Are you sure it's for me?"

He smiled, the wonder on her face tugging at something inside him. "Is your favorite color purple?" He nodded at the lavender tank top covering her thin frame.

"Yes. But how did the person know what color I liked?"

He glanced up at Hannah, who stood in the doorway, a file pressed to her belly as she watched the scene unfold.

"A little birdie told her."

Annie laughed and, in a quick move, tugged the hat down over her bare head, showing it was a perfect fit. "I can wear this under the hood on my winter coat."

"You can wear it whenever you want to. And you'll stay warmer than I will, as I don't have a special hat."

Hannah's teeth came down on her lip, and her

hand went behind her back. He only realized she was trying to find the doorknob when the door opened and she slid through it and around the corner. Was she crying?

Pregnancy hormones.

Even as the thought pressed in on him, he rejected it. Hadn't his own eyes moistened when Martha Brookstone's daughter had come by the office a week ago with an update on her mother? The hospice had been wonderful to them, she'd said. "Mom is weaker, but still insists on knitting hats for your patients." When she'd seen Annie in the waiting room she'd told her mother about her, and Martha had used some of her precious remaining energy to knit one last hat. She'd passed away yesterday morning, but her daughter had brought the hat in anyway, insisting her mother would have wanted Annie to have it.

His throat tightened with sadness and frustration. He hated cancer. Fought it with every ounce of strength he had, and yet it was never enough. He couldn't save every patient, no matter how hard he threw himself into his job.

He'd barely made it back to his office for his Saturday appointments after spending the morning in bed with Hannah. While the sex had been amazing, the closeness hadn't lasted longer than it had taken her to retrieve her clothes. She'd gotten up and showered, then slid out the door and out of his life.

Well, not out of his life because she was still here at the office a week later. But they'd both kept their distance, neither speaking about what had happened between them. In fact, Hannah was the consummate professional. Cool as a cucumber.

He should be glad. But he wasn't. He'd rather she came at him in a fury, asking what the hell he thought he was playing at.

Only he had no idea. All he knew was that whatever it was, it felt like fire…and silk. At the same time. Seducing him even while it burned him to the core. Hannah had hit the nail on the head: it was like playing with matches…thousands of them.

He brought his attention back to Annie and her mother. "That hat looks perfect on you."

Annie's mom smiled. "Tell the angel who knitted this we said thank you."

Greg wasn't about to tell her that Annie's "angel" had earned her wings and flown away, never to return.

He set up the next appointment and made sure the treatments were still on track. The child hugged him around the waist before she and her mother left, the fuzzy strands of the hat waving as she bounced her way down the hall. A very different little girl from the pale, despondent soul who'd sat silently in her chair.

Maybe he should see if he could find someone to knit hats for him on commission. If they could raise one person's spirits, it was worth it—because he was certain, no matter what the scientific world might say, the mind did play a role in a patient's recovery. Sometimes the illness was too great, but finding ways to rev up the immune system was a good thing. And if a simple hat could do that, then he was all for it.

Hannah came wandering down the hallway, another chart in her hands. "How'd it go?" she asked.

"You saw. She loved it." He paused. "You know, I've been thinking, maybe we could find someone who could knit those on a regular basis."

"That's a great idea. I used to knit, maybe I could—"

"No."

She frowned. "What?"

"I'm not putting anything more on you right now." He should have kept quiet about the idea, but he'd never expected her to immediately raise her hand and offer.

"You're not putting anything on me, Greg. I'm volunteering. Once I get home at night, I don't have all that much to do. Knitting would be a welcome distraction. I just need to practice to get back in the swing of things."

"You should be resting, not taking on more work. Especially now." His glance went to her stomach, trying to banish the thought that he knew exactly how it looked without a stitch of clothing. "When's your next doctor's appointment?"

"In a couple of weeks. She wants to do an ultrasound and check the position of the baby because I was on fertility drugs."

He glanced down the hallway to make sure no one was around, remembering Hannah saying she didn't want anyone to know yet. "What do the drugs have to do with position?"

There was a pause, and her cheeks lit up like red balloons. "Well…she wants to make sure there's only one."

"One?" A light bulb flashed inside his skull, blinding him for a second. Of course. Fertility drugs could cause more than one egg to be released. Oh, hell. "She thinks you're carrying more than one?"

She stepped closer and put a hand on his arm, making him realize his voice had risen to match his skyrocketing blood pressure. "Relax, she doesn't think anything at this point. She goes through the same procedure on all her fertility patients."

Relax? That was kind of hard when his brain was filtering through all kinds of scenarios. None of them good. What if Hannah did end up carrying more than one? What did that mean for him?

A nightmare, that's what. One that was increasing exponentially.

Even as he thought it, the opposite picture rose in his mind of Hannah propped up in bed with a baby in each arm, smiling up at him. There was a diamond on her left hand and the babies were a melding of their mother's facial features and his. Once inside his head, the image took hold, looking nothing like the nightmare he'd imagined.

Instead, the idyllic scene looked like a dream come true.

CHAPTER FOURTEEN

THE hat was lopsided, the lump along one side taking on the appearance of an ear flap, rather than a smooth round head covering. Maybe she could make one for her own baby this way.

Except there was no guarantee she could replicate the mistake—or have it come out the same for each ear. She needed a pattern to do that.

Hannah sighed and ripped the stitches out until she reached the part where things had first gone wonky, counting the rows carefully. The circular needles made for a seamless construction, which meant she wouldn't have to sew it together at the end, but keeping track of where she'd decreased her stitches was also more complicated. And she was only using regular knitting yarn right now. If she wanted to make those furry hats that were all the rage, it was going to be even harder because that kind of yarn had a lot of fringy fibers. Maybe Greg was right, she shouldn't be taking this on. Except hearing the constant click of the needles soothed her in a way that her own thoughts couldn't nowadays.

What Greg didn't know wouldn't hurt him. And once she brought in her first finished hat, he'd be so impressed with her talents that he wouldn't say another word.

Right. So why hadn't she just barreled her way through that disagreement and stood her ground? Because it had been easier not to. And she didn't like fighting with him.

Yes, she liked doing other things with him instead. Just the memory of that day they'd spent together made her stomach tighten. He had gone slow that second time. And by the end she'd been quaking with need and asking him to hurry all over again. He had, and the result had been an experience that still had the power to wake her up at night and turn her into a blathering idiot when she saw him at the office day after day.

What did that make her?

Infatuated.

He was the doctor who had treated her during her cancer scare. When she'd hugged him all those months ago, her heart had zigged when it should have zagged, sending her to a place she didn't want to be. Wasn't that what this was all about? She saw it happen time and time again with patients. They got a crush on the person they credited with saving their lives.

And if anyone deserved all that adulation, it was Greg.

Only it wasn't right for her to add one more set of doe eyes onto an already overburdened doctor.

Except, as far as she knew, he'd never shown a hint of attraction for any other of his patients, not even Claire Taylor—for whom she knew Greg had a soft spot.

Instead, he'd been a perfect gentleman during her treatments.

All it had taken was one weak moment on both their parts to start an avalanche neither of them seemed capable of stopping.

But she had to. He'd made it plain he didn't want a wife and a family no matter what he'd said during their last encounter. Besides, what had he said exactly? That he hadn't wanted a child…until the thought of this one being his had messed with his head?

So he hadn't wanted a family, until one had been forced on him.

Maybe his whole overdeveloped sense of responsibility had switched itself on and tricked him into thinking he wanted the baby. As a way to make him step up to the plate.

That was the last thing Hannah wanted. Especially as her own feelings about her boss were jumbled and confused.

If she wasn't careful, her heart could be snared in a trap of its own making. And then where would she be? In love with a man who could never truly love her back—whose desire to honor his sister's memory eclipsed anything but the need to work for a cause.

Laying the knitting needles in her lap, she set her wooden rocking chair into motion, closing her eyes and gripping the armrests. But Greg's face was right there, smiling down at her as he told her he had better places for her to kiss. The tenseness of his jaw as he'd finally reached the limits of his control and let go.

Her lips curved at the memories and then her eyes popped open.

Oh, no!

What if it wasn't infatuation at all? What if she really did have feelings for him? Big, honkin', end-of-the-line feelings that wouldn't simply go away once the baby was born?

Her hands went to her stomach, pleading with

all she had in her that her heart not go in that direction.

But it was hopeless. Her mind and her heart never saw eye to eye when it came to stuff like this. Her heart had wanted this baby while her mind had argued that she needed to wait a few years to be sure that her cancer really was gone for good.

Her heart had won in that instance.

Lord. She couldn't afford to let it win now. Not with everything that was at stake. The last thing her child needed once it was born was the tumultuous push and pull of an unstable relationship—one where she and Greg devoured each other one minute and avoided each other the next.

Neither did she want to end up as the "booty call" for a man who didn't have the emotional energy to nurture a relationship until it could withstand the wear and tear of normal life.

She deserved more than that. So did her child.

So what did she do? Find another job? Put her foot down and tell Greg that she was done with anything outside a professional working relationship.

The silence in her head was deafening.

Gee, thanks for the advice.

Picking up her knitting needles, she put one

point through the first of the row of stitches and threw the yarn over them. For now, all she could do was knit and hope that—like the screwball stitches she'd just ripped out—she could go back undo the mistakes she'd made with Greg and start all over.

Only she had a feeling that returning to an earlier time was going to be a whole lot easier to accomplish with yarn that it would be with Greg.

A hat.

Greg had to look twice before he realized what the item in the brown paper gift bag was. There was a little card on the handle that listed the name of a patient—Dorothy Acres. There was no indication who had sent it, although he had a sneaking suspicion.

So three days after he'd asked her not to take up knitting, she was already churning out hats. Who knew how many hours she'd burned through, doing this?

He hadn't seen much of her as he'd spent the past couple of days in surgery at the hospital. He'd just gotten back from one, in fact, and had decided to write up his notes while they were still fresh in his mind. He'd closed his office door to have some privacy.

It wasn't like he was intentionally avoiding her.

But there was a kernel of discontent lodged inside his gut that just wouldn't go away, no matter how many antacids he'd consumed over the past couple of days. He'd stripped his bed and washed the sheets on the hot-water setting of his machine, trying to pretend he was washing away his own misplaced sentiments right along with the reminder of their time together. Like when he'd replaced his old desk?

It hadn't worked then, and it didn't work now. Finding the hat only augmented his irritability. And the thought of her sitting at home all by herself with a pair of knitting needles wasn't helping any. Because his nights had been spent alone, as well.

That had never bothered him. Until now.

He'd had women before—not every weekend, or even every month, but often enough to know that something was off with his reactions to this situation. It had to be the pregnancy. Or maybe it was just Hannah herself.

Bethany would have liked her. Would have liked Hannah's spark of life, the way she always tried to do the right thing, rather than just making it easy on herself.

He shoved his chair away from the desk and stood, picking up his phone.

He paged Stella and waited for her to pick up. "Is Hannah still here somewhere?"

"Um, I think she's with a patient," his receptionist said, as if that fact should be obvious to even a simpleton like him.

Okay, so the sarcasm was probably a product of his own guilt and nothing to do with Stella dissing him. "When you see her, could you ask her to come to my office?"

As soon as he put the phone down he cursed himself as an idiot. Hannah had not set foot in his office since their fiery encounter there six weeks ago.

Six weeks. Had it been that long?

He counted back. It had.

Hannah had gone from bringing him coffee every day to avoiding him as much as he appeared to be avoiding her.

Although, someone had put that bag in his office. He somehow doubted it was Hannah.

The last thing he needed today, though, was for her to stand in front of his new desk while he sat behind it and pictured her sprawled across it all over again. He quickly picked up the gift bag and his patient's file and went over to the sitting area on the other side of the room. There, that was better. They could still see the desk but they wouldn't have to look across it in order to have a quick conversation.

And he intended this to be a quick, non-emotional session that put both their minds at ease.

A knock sounded at the door. He frowned. It had been a rare day when his PA didn't just open the door and come in. Just like on that fateful day when he'd gotten the news about Mrs. Brookstone.

"Come in." He laid the file on the coffee table, letting it remain open, as if he'd just been casually reviewing it.

Hannah poked her head inside, but didn't enter. "You wanted to see me?"

His irritation grew. If he could handle this like an adult, then so could she, dammit. "Would you mind coming in for a minute?"

You could have heard a pin drop in the silence that stretched between them. Finally, Hannah pushed through the door, making no effort to close it behind her. It was a telling move.

Was it him she didn't trust? Or herself?

That was a very dangerous question, and one he preferred not to answer right now.

He motioned to one of the wingback chairs that sat across from the leather sofa. Once she'd perched on the edge of it, her eyes went to the gift bag. So she already had an idea why he'd called her in. He nodded toward it. "Is this from you?"

"Does it matter?"

"I think you just answered my question. Didn't I say I didn't want you knitting hats?"

Her eyes narrowed slightly, she leaned back in her chair. "Were you ordering me not to make them or just suggesting that I shouldn't?"

A good question. He'd asked her not to, but was he so stupid as to think he could tell her how to spend her free hours and expect her to roll over and obey? Someone like Hannah? Not bloody likely.

Then what had he been doing?

He thought he'd been showing concern for her health. The baby's health. "It was a suggestion."

She nodded. "Okay. I found it…comforting."

She'd found what comforting? The suggestion or the knitting itself?

"I'm sorry, I don't follow."

"It gives me something constructive to do without brooding over the future."

The bald words reminded him of the ones she'd

uttered at his house. Was she really that worried about a possible relapse? Or was she worried that she might be stuck with him as the father of her child and wondering how much interference she'd get from him?

He leaned forward, planting his elbows on his knees, his chin on his fisted hands. "What part of the future?"

She shrugged, cheeks turning pink. "About the babie—baby. Whether or not everything will go okay with the pregnancy."

Had she been about to say "babies," plural? Was she actually expecting the doctor to find more than one during her next appointment? His mouth went dry.

"Did your doctor give you some cause for concern?"

"No, but you never know what could happen."

True. But other than finding multiple fetuses, Hannah was young and healthy. Her cancer was unlikely to return. She'd been able to get pregnant with the eggs she carried in her body, rather than the ones she'd frozen. It seemed like the odds were lining up in her favor. Then why wasn't she meeting his eyes? Was she still worried about Bethany's myeloid leukemia being passed down? If so, he could at least set her mind at ease regarding that.

"I talked to Bill Watterson a couple of days ago. He confirmed my family isn't one of those that carry the defective gene. So there's no chance of me passing it down."

"That's good. I wasn't worried, though."

But something was bothering her. He could see it in her face.

"Are you afraid I might interfere with the way you'll raise this child?"

She gave a soft laugh that sounded anything but happy. "Nope."

"What if it's mine?"

"What if it is?"

The words came out sounding like a challenge rather than an honest question—a kind of "so what are you going to do about it?" message.

He decided to tread softly. "What would you like me to do?"

"Nothing."

If he was closer, he'd reach out and take her hand. Touch her knee. Do something other than lean across a damn coffee table and try to get her to look at him—to really meet his eyes. "Do you want a marriage proposal?"

Her "No!" came at the exact same time his mind shouted, *What the hell are you doing?*

The horror in her voice, though, was a thousand times louder than his own. Because while he'd had this same inner tussle several times over the past couple of weeks, his heart had given a weird kind of sigh at his words. Like it might actually like the idea.

Well, *she* didn't. That much was obvious.

Hannah's words came tumbling out a second later, and she leaped to her feet. "Yes, I brought in the hat. And I want to make more of them, if that's okay with you. If it's not, I'll give them to the girls in the chemo room and let them hand them out as they see fit."

He got up as well and rounded the table until he stood in front of her. "Hey, I'm not going to stop you. If it makes you happy, by all means you should continue."

"Thank you."

He couldn't keep his eyes from trailing over her, acknowledging to himself that he was glad to finally see her up close, rather than just passing her in the hall for a few brief seconds. Despite the awkwardness currently between them, he missed having her barge in with a cup of coffee in the mornings. Missed the questions about whether or not he'd eaten lunch…or dinner. Missed her concern when a patient took a turn for the worse. But most of all he missed the easy camaraderie they used to have. It seemed like ages since they'd sat down and smiled and laughed like a couple of…

Friends.

Was that what he'd thought of her as?

Yes. Someone who knew who he was and who was perfectly okay with his shortcomings, with the energy he put into his job.

He wanted to tell her, but his throat felt paralyzed, unable to utter anything but meaningless questions.

"How many patients do we have left today?" Like that one. Meaningless. Not at all what he wanted to say.

She glanced at her watch. "I think two, why?"

Why? Because he wanted to see her. Spend time with her. And not just inside the bedroom—although he knew that was part of it. A big part. But he also wanted to hear about how her pregnancy was going and to know how she felt about it. Wanted her to want him to be a part of it.

But most of all he wanted to know where he fit into the scheme of things.

Suddenly he knew just the way to ask.

"After you have the baby, are you planning to come back to the clinic?"

CHAPTER FIFTEEN

"I don't know."

Hannah wasn't sure exactly how it had happened, but after the last patient left she found herself in Greg's car, the heater running as they discussed her work status at a nearby park. It was too chilly to get out and walk, and neither one of them had suggested going to get something to eat.

The thought of leaving the clinic caused something cold and hard to lodge in her throat, but she had no idea how she'd feel about working for Greg if the baby turned out to be his.

"What if I told you I don't want you to leave?"

A spark of joy leaped within her, only to fizzle out again. Was this the same type of offer as the "proposal" he'd mentioned earlier? Born of a sense of responsibility? He didn't want her as his wife so how did she know he still wanted her at the clinic?

"Is this because you somehow feel responsible for knocking me up? Because if it is—"

"Please don't use that term."

She blinked. Somehow she'd assumed that was all this was to him. A mistake. One that never should have happened. Hadn't he said as much?

No, actually, he hadn't. But surely he'd thought it. *She* had. "Sorry."

"And no, this isn't about feeling responsible, although I do, to some extent. But you're good for the clinic. Good for our patients."

Right. The cynical part of her mind gave her heart a knowing wink. Hadn't it told her that all along?

Before she could open her mouth to respond, he shook his head. "No, that's a lie. You are good for the clinic, but you're also good for me. You drag me back to earth when I've gotten my head too far up my…" He cleared his throat. "Too far in the clouds."

She couldn't stop her laugh. "I think I liked your first attempt better."

He smiled back at her. "See? You're also good for my ego."

"You mean by chopping it back down to a manageable size?" She relaxed in her seat, swiveling her knees toward him so she could look at him.

"Exactly." His face turned serious as he studied her. "I've missed this."

"So have I."

They looked at each other for a few more seconds, before Hannah glanced away. "If this baby does turn out to be yours, don't you think things could become strained?"

"Only if we let them."

Her brows went up. "Seriously? Look at us now, at the clinic. You can barely stand to talk to me."

"It's hard, I admit. But we could work through it."

Pain lodged in her chest and branched out, like crystals forming in a jar of sugar water. He'd just admitted to avoiding her. Was that why his hours at the hospital had suddenly increased? She'd gone from being a collaborator on cases to handling some of them on her own, just going to him for a quick consult when she was unsure of something. Was that how she wanted to continue? It gave her a lot more freedom to make decisions, but she liked the give and take as they'd brainstormed through problems. Instead, she felt like she'd been set adrift.

It was a lonely feeling. Maybe that's why she suddenly looked to knitting as a type of therapy. She'd even finished a brown argyle beanie hat, the pattern for which she'd found in a magazine. They didn't have any male patients at the moment, yet her fingers had found their way to that page time and time again, carefully selecting the shades and the layout—matching the color of Greg's hair. The finished product had come out just as she'd imagined.

You'll stay warmer than I will, as I don't have a special hat. The words he'd said to Annie when he'd given her Martha's gift ran through her mind. Something about them had grabbed hold of her throat and squeezed tight, which was ridiculous. He'd just been making idle conversation.

So why had the words stuck with her? It's not like she'd ever have the courage to give it to him.

"Are you sure you wouldn't rather just get a new PA?" The question sounded as shaky as her legs had become.

His brows came together. "Would I be sitting here in the damn car, asking you to stay, if I did?"

Why the sudden flare of anger? Maybe the thought of her leaving really did bother him.

"What would you do while I was on maternity leave?"

He took a minute to think about that. "I could cut back on my patient load until you got back."

"What? You always say that, but know you'd never be able to."

"I already have, remember? It's why you're able to leave here by six o'clock every night, rather than eight."

She pounced on those words. "Ha! I know for a fact you sneak patients in after everyone's gone home." Several mornings she'd come in to find the paper on the exam tables rumpled from someone's body and had had to strip them before beginning a new day. She was pretty sure Greg wasn't snoozing on them at night. Not when he had that long couch in his office. And that comfy bed in his home.

Something she'd better avoid thinking about.

"You do? How?"

She tapped her forehead. "I'm psychic."

"Well, I wouldn't have a choice when you're gone. I'd have to cut back. I can't be at the hospital and the clinic at the same time."

He was right, he couldn't be two places at once. Which was why the thought of being married to someone like him was beyond absurd.

"That's true. You can't be." She heard the wistfulness in her voice and cringed inwardly. But maybe Greg hadn't noticed. He probably had too much on his mind to notice the subtle shift in pitch…the note of sorrow she'd unintentionally injected.

His throat moved, then his hand came out to squeeze hers. "I'm trying to do better, Hannah."

That was the problem. No matter how much he might want to change, he wouldn't. Not really. Not until he could temper whatever drove him to work so hard and so long. Only Greg knew if the compulsion was out of control or if he really could back away from it. Hannah loved the patients she treated, but she also knew there was a limit to how much she could do before her body and mind rebelled.

Greg's never seemed to, although she had no idea how he could stay focused for as long as he did.

But, like he'd said, he didn't have anyone else to worry about. And that's the way he liked it.

"It's not a matter of doing better. It's a matter of taking care of yourself, so that you can take care of others. You don't eat right. You probably don't sleep well. When I was at your house, your refrigerator was practically empty."

Instead of taking offense, he laughed. "Thanks."

Huh?

"For what?"

"For fussing at me. You haven't done that in a

while." He linked his fingers through hers. "Like I said, I've missed it."

Things between them *had* been strained lately. And she hadn't been in his office in a while. Was it possible he'd liked what they'd had before?

She squeezed his hand back. "So have I."

"So you'll at least think about staying once the baby is born?"

"Yes. I'll think about it."

"I appreciate it." He let out a huge breath. "I can't promise I'll be able to change overnight, but I'll at least try."

Maybe she'd been wrong. Maybe he really *would* try to make time for things outside work. A ball of hope formed in her chest.

"Promise?"

"I do."

The doctor stared at the ultrasound monitor, a frown of concentration on her face.

Hannah's anxiety level had been going up in steady increments for the past ten minutes. This was taking a lot longer than she'd expected. At eight weeks Dr. Preston should be able to find the baby and see its tiny heart pumping, even if she couldn't find it on the Doppler yet. "Is everything okay?"

"Just give me another minute here."

The same answer the doctor had given her the last time she'd asked. What if the baby was dead?

Her own heart stalled at the thought.

Greg had offered to come with her, but their patient load was heavy today and she hadn't felt right about dragging him away. Especially as he had been better about eating. They'd even started meeting in his office for coffee again in the mornings, like they used to.

And most days Greg had already poured and doctored hers up with creamer and sugar before she even got to the office, which was different from the way it had been before. Stella would just nod toward the door and send her on her way.

And now she was alone in a room, possibly about to hear the worst news of her life.

"Hannah, there're two of them."

"Two what?" Heads? Torsos? Babies…?

"You're going to have twins. Sorry for taking so long. I wanted to be sure before I said anything." She turned the monitor toward Hannah.

"Twins?" She'd known this was a possibility.

Barb had even warned her ahead of time, but to actually hear the word was…

Terrifying.

Two babies. How could that be?

"You're positive."

"I am." She pointed out the babies, one of which appeared to be superimposed over the other. "The angle made it hard to see. I wanted to make sure they weren't fused."

"Oh, God. They're not, are they?" Conjoined twins would send her soul plummeting back to earth.

"No. There are two separate individuals in there. Oh, and they're fraternal, as there are two placentas."

"It's just so… I'll have to…"

To what? Tell Greg? Oh, no. Her fear grew even more. What was she going to tell him? He'd freaked out over one baby, what would he do with the news that he might have fathered two?

Maybe he hadn't.

"Any chance of knowing if these are the result of the insemination?"

Dr. Preston squeezed her shoulder. "No, sorry. There's no way to tell for sure until we do a D.N.A.

test, and you said you wanted to wait on that, right?"

"Yes." She had. And Greg's quiet words came back to her, affirming it was the right decision. He hadn't wanted her to risk losing the baby just to put his mind at ease.

But now that there were two? Would he still feel the same way?

She gulped as another thought hit her. "You're positive there aren't any more in there, right?"

The doctor laughed. "Yes. I'm sure. I almost missed the second one as it was."

Maybe it would have been better if the second baby had remained hidden a little while longer. She and Greg were just getting back on solid footing. But withholding this kind of information wouldn't do anyone any good. And if he'd been able to come to her appointment, like he'd wanted to, he would already know.

Yes, she had to tell him.

But when?

Um, yeah. Like he wouldn't ask how the appointment had gone the second she got back to the office. Nothing to do but suck it up and tell the truth.

She got back during the lunch lull, which was both fortunate and unfortunate as it didn't give her much of a chance to prepare. Nonetheless, there was no time like the present. Armed with two fresh cups of coffee, she made her way to Greg's office, mumbling the words she wanted to say under her breath. She slid one mug in the crook of her elbow and knocked, heard his "Come in" and took a deep, deep breath before taking that final step.

If she'd been hoping he was immersed in paperwork and would give her a few more minutes, she was mistaken. He was sitting behind his desk, elbows propped on the flat, empty surface, staring off into space.

Brooding over his lot in life?

Lord, she hoped not, because it was about to get a whole lot worse.

She held out a cup. "I made a fresh pot."

Nodding an acknowledgment, he accepted it and took a fairly big sip. Bracing himself. Great. Brooding *and* bracing.

He set the cup on the desk. "How is he?"

"He?"

"The baby, sorry. Just using the generic term… unless you already know what it is?"

"I don't know the sex yet, no." She licked suddenly dry lips. "But I did learn something pretty significant."

A frown appeared. "Did a problem show up on the sonogram?"

The worried note in his voice made her rush ahead. "Oh, no. There's nothing wrong with... them."

He blinked. Stared. His Adam's apple took at least one dive, possibly two, before he said in a low controlled voice, "Them?"

"Yes."

"Them, as in more than one fetus?"

"Yes."

He leaned back in his chair, the springs protesting the sudden change. Then, as if he needed to distance himself even farther from the news, he swiveled half a turn to the left until he faced the wall. Planting his elbows on his knees, he closed his eyes and pressed his fingertips into his temples. His face was paler than she'd ever seen it. Hannah wondered for a moment if he was going to be physically sick.

"Greg? Are you okay?"

One hand left his temple to wave a warning, which she took to mean he needed another minute or two.

Oh, Lordy. She was beginning to feel a little

nauseated herself, nerves causing her stomach to froth and twist.

He'd known this might be a possibility, so why was he acting as if it was a death sentence?

Then, in case he might be wondering, or might be trying to get up the nerve to ask, she forced herself to say, "I'm not going to ask about a reduction."

"Of course not."

He still hadn't moved. Hannah couldn't tell whether the words were meant as an affirmation or an indictment. Or maybe he was simply resigning himself to his fate.

She tried to explain. "I can't, Greg. Twins are easily managed, and if something should happen to one of them, I...I..." Even the thought brought a quick slice of pain.

He turned back toward her. "I wasn't asking you to."

She hesitated, trying to feel him out. "I know this must come as a shock."

"You have no idea."

He picked up a pencil and toyed with it as she searched for something else to say. Something that might make him feel at least a little better.

"They might not be yours, you know."

He set the pencil down with a click. "I'm going to assume they are, until I know otherwise."

He was? Why? He was obviously not overjoyed with the news. It would be so much easier to grab the lifeline she'd handed him and pull himself to shore—far from the likes of her and the babies. So why wasn't he?

Because that wasn't the way Greg did things. Not in his line of work. He evaluated the situation, identified the worst-case scenario and then fought to improve the odds. But this time there was no way to change course. What was done was done. They couldn't go back and undo it.

She almost laughed. Although Greg had certainly given it a shot by banishing the old desk and getting a light pine mission-style thing that clashed with all the other ornate mahogany pieces. If his decorator could see it, she'd cringe. She had to admit, though, it was a relief not to have to face him over that other desk or something that was almost like it.

"Maybe that's not a wise thing to do. If they end up not being yours, won't you be…?"

Sad?

No, of course he wouldn't be. He'd be hugely relieved, just like she would.

Wouldn't she? The empty place in her chest said otherwise.

"Will I be upset? Maybe. But things would be a whole lot less complicated."

That was one point they could definitely agree on. "Yes, they would."

He dragged a hand through his hair. "Any other exciting news you'd like to spring on me?"

"I did ask Dr. Preston if she was sure there weren't any more hiding in there."

He coughed, then cleared his throat. The first hint of a smile finally made its way across his face. "And?"

"There aren't. She almost missed the second one as it was. He or she was hiding behind the first baby."

"Probably afraid of my reaction." His gaze finally landed on her face. "And I'm sorry for that." He hesitated. "Are you happy?"

She searched inside herself and found the answer. "Yes."

"Congratulations, Hannah." He leaned across his desk and held out his hand, waiting until she took it. "When are they due again?"

"July twelfth."

He squeezed her fingers then released them. "They don't usually let twins go to term, do they?"

"No. Dr. Preston said to plan for thirty-seven weeks."

"So now you have two baby names to come up with instead of just one."

"Ye-es." She drew the word out, wondering if she should do this now or let him recover a little while longer. But he seemed softer and more relaxed, even if he wasn't shouting for joy. She'd been holding on to the question for the last week, trying to get the nerve up—and that had been when she'd thought there was only one baby.

What if he laughed in her face or, worse, shouted for her to get out of his office? Well, nothing could be worse than the way he'd shut down on her a few minutes ago. At least, she hoped not.

Taking a deep breath, she forged ahead. "Can I get your opinion on something?"

He picked up his coffee and took another sip. A shorter one this time. "Sure."

Setting her own cup in her lap, she wrapped both hands around it, noting that the now-tepid brew was still warmer than her icy fingers.

"If one of the babies is a girl, what do you think about naming her Bethany, after your sister?"

CHAPTER SIXTEEN

His sister?

Greg wasn't sure he'd heard the words correctly—in fact, he wasn't sure he'd heard *anything* correctly for the past fifteen minutes—so he sat there trying to replay that last sentence. But all that kept running through his head was the word *twins*.

"Could you repeat that?"

"It's fine if you don't want to. I mean, I know it's really soon, so feel free to take some time to think it over before you—"

"You don't even know if the babies are mine. Why would you want to do that?"

"Because your sister was obviously a beautiful person. She's the reason you fight so hard for your patients. What a wonderful legacy. And if you decide never to have children of your own..." She shrugged, not quite meeting his eyes. "It's something I've been thinking about for the past week or so."

Hannah was right. He did fight for his patients,

but only because Bethany had taught him how to—had always been the one person he could count on to understand. Just as Hannah seemed to, first at his house and now right here in this very office.

Hell. Something was wrong. Hannah's face blurred and then came back into sharp focus. The problem wasn't with her features, though, it was with his eyes. There was a layer of moisture over them that was growing deeper by the second.

Another happy little girl might carry Bethany's name. The problem with his eyes had now spread to his lungs, which burned with every breath he took.

Getting up from his seat, he went to the window and stared out over the parking lot, scrubbing his hand over his face. Last week's dusting of snow had melted but the sky was overcast.

A gentle hand landed on his shoulder. "I'm sorry I upset you. I won't do it, if you don't want me to, if it would hurt too much."

Half turning, he wrapped his arms around her and laid his cheek on top of her head, her soft scent filling his chest. Despite his attempts to dash them away, the damned mist covered his eyes again, this time spilling onto Hannah's hair.

He took a deep shuddery breath, fighting to get himself under control. "It doesn't upset me. I don't think anyone has ever done a nicer thing for me or for Bethany. Thank you."

Her arms circled his waist, and she rested her head on his chest. "You're welcome."

For the first time, the idea of kids and a family didn't send his heart racing into a state of panic or make him shy away in horror. Instead, as he stood in his office, holding Hannah in his arms, a sense of rightness flowed through him.

He loved her.

How? When?

He had no idea. The realization hadn't hit him like a bolt from the sky. Neither did it bring an unwelcome jolt of surprise. It was something that had begun growing the moment she'd thrown her arms around him and thanked him at the end of her treatments, her soft scent sweeping through him then just as it did now, her trembling body awaking something in his heart. Or maybe it had started even before that.

Yes, he was terrified. He hadn't planned on falling in love any more than he'd planned on fathering twins. But the feeling was there, and he could at least admit it to himself for this one moment in time, even if he never did anything about it.

"I have something else to ask." Hannah's voice was muffled by his shirt.

What else could she throw at him besides twins and wanting to name one of them after Bethany?

"What is it?"

"If the babies end up being yours…" She paused for a long second before continuing. "And if my cancer comes back at some point, I want to make preparations in advance. Do you have any preferences about who should raise them?"

If her cancer came back…

A black spot opened up in his chest at the thought.

Nothing would happen to Hannah. He'd make sure of it.

Like he had his sister?

"You're going to be fine. The cancer's not going to recur." Hodgkin's was different from his sister's disease. It had a high cure rate.

"You can't know that for sure. No one does. I just don't want to leave things up in the air. If they're yours, you should have a say about where they go."

Just like he knew he loved her, Greg's heart whispered the answer that had been there all along.

"I'll raise them."

"What?" Her head came off his chest, and she looked up at him.

"I said I'll raise them."

He wouldn't have to, though. Hannah was going to be around for a long time to come. She'd raise her children and wave them off to college. But she wasn't asking for reassurances. She was making arrangements, it was as simple as that. And this was the right thing to do.

He gave an inward smile. *See, Bethany? I can do it.*

"Are you sure?" Hannah asked. "You're so busy, and that is a huge commitment."

He searched around inside himself. He could ask his parents for help—his mother would be thrilled, and maybe it would help to heal the rift between him and his father. He could even move his practice to Ketchikan to be closer to them if necessary. But the thought of Hannah no longer being on this earth…

Then don't think about it. Just answer her question.

"I'm sure." He paused. "What if they're the donor's children? Are your parents well enough to handle raising two children?"

"Yes. They're both still fairly active. But they're in Idaho, so the children would have to go there."

Idaho.

The lower forty-eight always seemed like another world to someone who'd been born and raised in Alaska. And Idaho was three thousand miles away. So he'd probably never see the twins again.

"Let's not talk about this right now, okay?" He allowed his right hand to stroke along her spine. "I'm still getting used to the fact that there are two of them."

Hannah smiled. "Yeah, me too. All I can think about is what I'm going to look like when I'm eight months pregnant."

"You're going to look beautiful, just like you do now."

Her smile faded. "Thank you. That's a really sweet thing to say."

Before he could stop himself, he dropped a quick kiss on her lips. "It might be sweet, but it's also true." He sighed. "And as much as I don't want to, I'd better get out there before Stella sends someone in after me. Or, worse, comes looking for me herself. We might have some explaining to do in that case."

"Speaking of explaining..." Hannah dropped

her arms from his waist and took a step back. "I'm eventually going to have to tell everyone I'm pregnant. How do you want me to play it?"

He fingered the silver earring that dangled from a dainty lobe. "Play it by ear. Just like we've been doing with everything else."

Play it by ear.

That's what Hannah had done with his spontaneous kiss yesterday, and with his shocking offer to raise the twins should they prove to be his. And when he'd called her beautiful, her heart had almost stopped.

But she'd smiled as if it had meant nothing special, all the while wondering if his feelings for her might be growing. Just like hers were.

A very scary proposition when you considered it. Dropping the new gift bag on his desk, she ran her fingers along the wooden surface. Several patient files were now scattered across the top of it, unlike yesterday when it had been empty.

She hadn't wanted to fall for him. If she could go back and undo the sequence of events that had led her here, she would. She'd have continued calling him Dr. Mason and maintained that professional distance she seemed to need. At least with him. She'd never had any trouble calling other colleagues by their first names. But she'd resisted with Greg.

Now she knew why.

The door opened, and she jumped when the man himself appeared. "I thought you were at the hospital."

"I was. I finished up early."

"You did?" With the way Greg lived his life, she'd never have considered letting him raise these children.

Until he'd cried.

Oh, he didn't know she'd felt the moisture in her hair, and she hadn't dared say anything. But at that moment she'd known he could love them, if it came down to it. Known he'd sacrifice everything for them, the same way he'd made sacrifices in his sister's memory.

She pulled her mind away from those thoughts as he came into the room and closed the door behind him.

"I only had two patients." He smiled. "And, yes, I checked the chemo room. No one there from our practice."

Our. That was the first time he'd ever used that term.

Hannah motioned toward the desk. "I've gotten another hat done." And his still sat in a little bag on her dining room table. She would eventually have to give it to him. What was the worst he could do? Laugh and think her silly?

"That's two hats this week. You're going to run through all our patients within a month or two."

His words were light, but Hannah didn't smile. "We'll always have new ones."

"Yes, unfortunately." He took another step toward her, sliding his fingers beneath her chin. "Are you okay?"

She scrabbled around for something to say. "Just feeling a bit melancholy today, for some reason."

"You need to get away for a little while." He glanced at his watch. "Do you have plans this weekend?"

Yes. Knitting. Staring at her fish. Pining after her boss. Full schedule. "Nope. Just relaxing."

The fingers beneath her chin trailed along her jawline, sending a shiver over her. "My folks have a little vacation cabin about an hour north of here. I was thinking about going up there." He paused. "Are you interested in joining me?"

He never left town, as far as she knew. What was behind his sudden need to clear out? "Since when do you leave for the weekend?"

"It's been ages since I've been up there. Maybe your moose encounter made me miss the woods. I don't know. I just know I'd like to head up there… and I'd like some company. We could talk about the babies and your plans for the future."

"M-my plans?"

He dropped his hand. "If you don't want to, it's fine."

"No, no, it's not that. You just surprised me." Her insides warred for a second or two, the "should" battling it out with the "want to," although there was never any doubt as to which side would win, really. "Thank you. I'd like to go."

"Great. Do you want to leave tonight or Saturday morning?"

"I need to pack, so could we make it tomorrow?"

"Sure."

Hannah thought she heard a note of disappointment in his voice, but surely not. He'd probably regret asking her as soon as she left the office. Maybe he'd even call to say he'd changed his mind.

"What time to you want to leave?"

"Is nine o'clock too early?"

"No, that's fine." Her head was whirling. She'd gone from wondering how she could have avoided this particular train wreck to agreeing to spend the weekend with him. It was probably reckless and wildly idiotic, but she wanted to go. Wanted to head somewhere private where they could talk through things for once, instead of wondering where all this was leading. "Does the cabin have heat?"

If not, she'd have to bring some additional layers.

"It does. It also has linens and towels and everything we'll need to cook meals. Except the food."

Cooking. She hadn't thought about that. "Do you want me to pick up some groceries?"

"I'll do that. Or we can eat out for lunch and dinner."

But not for breakfast. She remembered the omelet he'd made them. Remembered the events afterward. Suddenly she thought of something that should have been apparent from the outset. He planned on them sleeping together, obviously. Why else would he have asked her? The thought should have made her uneasy, since she'd already given herself the "booty call" lecture, but it didn't. Instead a stream of anticipation began swirling through her stomach.

"Oh, and, Hannah..." His fingers slid through

her hair, ruffling the short strands as he gave her a slow smile. "In case you're worried about my intentions, the cabin has two bedrooms."

CHAPTER SEVENTEEN

"IT'S beautiful!"

Greg smiled as Hannah gave a small twirl, taking in the rustic entryway of the log cabin. He dropped their bags on the plank floor, his worries over asking her to join him dissipating. If she'd turned him down, would he even be here?

Doubtful. His decision to come had been an impulsive one at best, and although he was antsy about being so far from Anchorage, he'd traveled to medical conferences in the past and nothing terrible had happened. The world had continued its slow, methodical turn. His absence hadn't spawned any natural disasters.

Besides, he'd wanted some time alone with her to try to figure this thing out and decide what he should do about it. What was it about her that drew him time and time again?

Who was Hannah, really?

He knew exactly who she was. A survivor who, like his sister, challenged him to be the best he could be. Hannah was also kind and caring and made his blood turn to fire the second she walked—or barged—into a room. A woman who might be carrying his children. She was already a professional partner, but could she be more than that? He'd gotten things a little backward, but maybe that's what it had taken to get through to him.

"I'm glad you like it." He went to a nearby wall and switched on the gas fireplace, even as he tried to see the place through her eyes. The foyer opened into a great room with sturdy leather furnishings and a rough pine table. He could remember his whole family coming up here during summer vacations—at least until he and his father had had that final big blowup. His mom had been surprised when he'd called, asking if they still had the place, but she'd been happy. The key was still in the same spot, she'd said. In that silly fake rock his father kept next to the front porch.

Hannah kept her coat on and made a beeline for the fireplace, holding her hands out. "Does this heat the whole house?"

"No, there's central heat as well, but this is a little more immediate."

"Brrr...I think winter is already moving in."

Frost had painted the landscape white that morning when he'd gone to pick her up, and the temperature hadn't warmed up much during the trip. No precipitation predicted, but the sky was grey and overcast. "You could be right."

Shrugging out of his heavy parka, he hung it on a hook in a nearby closet then picked up their bags again. "Which bedroom do you want?"

"Whichever one you don't want." She sank to her knees on the rug in front of the fireplace, sighing. 'I think I'm going to sit here for a minute or two and get warmed up. Where does it get its gas?"

"From a big tank out back. It should be fine for the time we're here. Do you want me to crank it up higher?"

"No, it feels wonderful. I could sit here all day."

So could he. Right next to her.

And as far as putting her bag in whichever room he *didn't* want, that was going to be a little tricky, because he'd immediately want to be in the one she was in. But that wasn't smart. He'd brought her here to be with her, to spend time with her. It was better to give her some space, not to mention the fact that he could do with some of that himself. Okay…easy solution. He'd give her his parents' room. That should put paid to any thoughts of sneaking into her bed in the middle of the night.

"I'll put these away and then see about lunch."

"Mmm. I'll help you in a few minutes. Once I thaw a bit more." She curled up on the rug in front of the fireplace, much as Bethany's cat would have done years ago.

Despite Hannah's words, she looked anything but frozen. He was sure if he touched her, she'd be warm and soft. Which was why he was heading straight to the bedrooms before he dropped onto the rug behind her and tucked her close.

Going first to the room he'd shared with Bethany when they'd been kids, he set his suitcase on the floor, staring at the place where the two single beds had been replaced with a queen-size one. He could still visualize the bedding and how she'd talked their parents into rigging a curtain to go between the beds so she could pretend to have her own room. The ceiling rod was gone, the area painted to look brand-new. In fact, the whole room had been redecorated, for which he was grateful. The outside wall was made of thick rustic logs, but the three inside walls had changed from pale yellow to nondescript beige. All traces of Bethany had been scrubbed clean. It was as if she'd never been here at all.

Only she had been. And, in a way, her presence was still here. It was one of the reasons he hadn't been to the place in years. But instead of the crippling sadness her memory had once dredged up, he found the pain had eased, even if it wasn't completely gone. He could now smile at the mischievous antics she'd once engaged in. Remember how happy this place had made her.

Something inside him relaxed. It was going to be okay.

Maybe that's why he'd needed to come. To get a sense of what his sister would have wanted him to do.

Hannah didn't want to marry him. Even if she hadn't said the words, her face had been a picture of shock and dismay when he'd mentioned it. Enough that he wouldn't pursue that avenue again. But it didn't have to be marriage, necessarily. Maybe she could grow to care for him—could trust him not only to raise her children in the event of her death but enough to let him be a part of her life, as well.

Was that what he wanted?

Yes. But he wasn't sure he could do it. Or whether

or not he should. This weekend was meant to be a test run. And a lot rode on how he felt by the end of it.

"Is this where I'll stay?" Hannah's voice yanked him from his thoughts. He knew she meant "stay" as in temporarily, but the word made something shift inside him. The urge to ask her to share the room with him came and went without incident. He shifted gears.

"Weren't you going to warm up for a while?"

"Already done." She put her hand on his. "See? Warm as toast."

Yes, it was. And he was growing a bit heated himself. He cleared his throat. "I'm going to put you in the room across the hall. There's only one bathroom, so we'll have to share. My parents always meant to add a second one, but they never got around to it." And once Bethany had died, there'd been no need, as they'd no longer come here as a family.

"Okay."

That reminded him. He'd have to switch on the hot-water heater and let it run for a couple of hours before they could shower. "Let me show you your room."

He made the trek across the narrow hallway, suddenly glad to be moving. Opening the door, he let her walk in ahead of him. The room was chilly, but he could already feel heat gusting from one of the overhead vents.

A soft exclamation of surprise came from behind her. "You should take this room."

He knew why she'd said it. This bedroom was obviously the master suite, since the huge four-poster bed dominated the space—his mother's one big splurge. A system of mahogany slats cleverly attached to the four carved finials, creating a canopy that could be disassembled depending on the mood.

His mother had always liked them up, had even bought a lacy fabric covering that was probably still tucked in one of the closets somewhere, but Greg liked the bare wood. "No, I'm fine in the other one. It's where I used to sleep as a child."

"But this bed is bigger. And you're—"

"Don't say it."

She grinned. "I wasn't going to say you're fat. You're not. But you are a big guy."

Her cheeks colored almost as soon as the words left her mouth. His cue to back out of there, and fast.

"Do you want to unpack?"

"I think I'm going to leave my things in the suit-case. We'll only be here for one night."

"Right." Suddenly it wasn't enough. He wanted a week. A month.

A lifetime?

Stick with the plan, Greg. Take it one day at a time.

"I'll bring the rest of the stuff in from the car."

"Want some help?" She stood in the doorway as if unsure what to do next.

"I've got it. I thought we might eat lunch here at the cabin and then do dinner at a seafood joint in town."

"Sounds good." She patted her tummy. "I ate breakfast, but I'm already starving. Must be the air up here."

He could blame the air for his ravenous appetite, but this was a completely different kind of hunger—one that physical food wouldn't put a dent in.

"I've brought steak and potatoes. How does that sound?"

"Like a little piece of heaven. I'm so glad I haven't had any morning sickness yet. I'm eating all I can, just in case it eventually hits." She put one hand on the edge of the door. "Oh, are there sheets already on the bed?"

"No, Mom used to keep them in the dresser drawers in each bedroom—they're probably still there, in a zippered bag. We can throw a set in the washer, and then I'll help you make the bed."

Her brows went up. "I have made a bed before, you know."

He did know. And that was something else he didn't want to think about. The way she looked as she bent over the exam tables, pulling paper from the roll and tucking it beneath the strap at the bottom. How her perfect behind had called out to him, inviting him to mess up the bed she'd so meticulously made. But then he might have had to buy a new exam table, for the very same reasons he'd gotten a new desk. That might be a little harder to explain to Stella.

His perceptive receptionist had eyed him with one brow raised nearly to her hairline as they'd carried his old desk away. The thing was still tucked in a storage area, awaiting his decision on what to do with it. He couldn't bear to throw it out. Maybe he should move it to his house. There wasn't much furniture in the place.

And see Hannah's slim body stretched across it every time he passed by? Yeah, if he thought he was tired now, he'd be doubly exhausted if he did that.

Since when had he gotten so sentimental?

Maybe since seeing on a daily basis how fragile the thread of life was. He'd learned to notice little things about his patients that he might have overlooked before, like the soft glances between Claire and her husband. Or hands that gripped tightly as he talked about their particular illness. Or…

"Greg? Are you okay?"

"Yep, fine." He rolled his shoulders to relax some of the tension. "Like I said, linens are in the drawer. Choose whichever set you like and bring them to the kitchen. The washer and dryer are in a closet next to the pantry."

"Okay." Her gaze trailed over his face as if trying to figure out what he'd been thinking about, but she didn't ask. "Do you want me to get out a set for you, as well?"

"Sure. I'll be back in a few minutes."

Greg hightailed it out of there before she figured out that she was part of his salva—confusion. Hell, had he almost used the word *salvation?* He didn't need anyone to save him. Unless it was from his own recent thoughts and actions.

He'd done some things that were pretty out of character for him.

Rescuing the grocery bags from the trunk of his car, he brought them in the house and quickly sorted through them. He glanced at his watch. Almost lunchtime. Good. At least the food preparations would keep him from doing any more thinking.

Because right now thinking was the one thing that could take an otherwise cautious and controlled doctor and turn him into a type of Mr. Hyde.

One who only wanted one thing out of this trip.

Hannah.

CHAPTER EIGHTEEN

SHE was crazy cold, but it was so worth it.

When Greg had said he had a surprise for her, she'd glanced at her watch and blinked. Almost midnight. But now, seated on the whitewashed porch swing overlooking the front yard, she curled up in a ball and hugged her knees. And stared.

Lights.

The gorgeous green hues of the aurora borealis hung high in the sky, a soft misting of color that was perfectly visible from her seat. The swing creaked as Greg sat beside her, tossing a throw from the couch over both their shoulders and wrapping it around them. "To keep us warm," he'd murmured, when she'd looked at him.

She was. His body heat, trapped within the folds of the woolen fabric, quickly made the nippy temperature more bearable, even for her feet, which normally turned into heavy blocks of ice whenever she sat outside for extended periods.

"How did you know it would happen tonight?"

she asked. You couldn't always predict when the lights would appear, and sometimes they only lasted for minutes before fading away again.

"I didn't. I glanced outside and there it was." He shifted on the seat, the move bringing him close enough that his shoulder slipped behind hers. She responded by leaning against him, automatically seeking the extra heat he was giving off. "This used to be Bethany's favorite part of coming to the cabin."

"Tell me about her." It wasn't often he volunteered information about his sister, and she was curious.

He shrugged. "She was feisty. Made me stand up to my dad when he wanted me to take over his fishing business."

"And you wanted to be a doctor."

"Yes." He gave a soft chuckle. "And Bethy nagged me until I told him the truth, that I didn't want to be a commercial fisherman. She knew I'd be miserable if I tried to force myself to be something I wasn't."

"That must have been tough." She couldn't imagine her parents pressuring her into taking over their cattle ranch. There'd never even been a hint that she should give up her own dreams and take on theirs.

"It was. Things have been shaky between my dad and I ever since." His arm went around Hannah's shoulders, drawing her closer. "But it was the right thing to do."

"I'm glad she insisted."

He paused, before saying, "Me, too."

She sighed, turning her attention back to the sky. "I think this is the clearest I've ever seen the lights. I've heard northern Idaho has displays from time to time, but I'm from the southern part of the state so I'd never experienced them before moving to the Aleutians. And then, after my diagnosis, there weren't a lot of opportunities."

The time she'd spent on the island of Dutch Harbor had been a magical, eye-opening period. The inhabitants knew how to make the most of what they had. She still missed the island, and her friends there.

Hmm… But not that much, she thought as she rested her head on Greg's shoulder. This was definitely something she could get used to. Sitting on a porch with him, watching the mysterious glow dance across the night sky, the silence broken only by the occasional shuffle of wildlife in the distance or the soft hoot of an owl in a nearby tree.

"I don't think I could ever get tired of seeing this."

Greg's warm breath slid across her cheek. "You don't get tired of it. But you do take it for granted. Forget it exists."

"Kind of like good health."

"Yes, unfortunately. In our practice we're suddenly more aware of things like the northern lights, aren't we?"

"Having cancer changes you. Sometimes for the better. Like appreciating the beauty of the lights, for example. You learn to treasure every second."

"Is that why you decided to have children?"

Hannah had sensed him wanting to talk about this earlier, but he'd never quite made it around to the subject. Maybe it was for the best. Because out here she felt a kind freedom she'd been longing for. "Yes. Putting it off until I met the right person just didn't seem like the best decision for me anymore."

"So you decided to go it alone."

"I was alone during my illness and treatment so this doesn't seem like such a huge step."

Warm lips touched her temple. "I'm sorry you felt alone. Your parents?"

"My mom came up for a couple of weeks, but when she realized she couldn't really help I talked her into going home. My dad gets nervous when he can't do something to make things better." She paused. "He's in the early stages of Parkinson's. It's another reason I didn't want to wait. I wanted my dad to be able to hold his grandchild while he's still well enough to."

"I didn't know."

She shrugged. "It's just something that's never come up between us."

"Anything else?"

"What do you mean?" She glanced up to see his eyes fixed on the lights.

"What about the twins? What are your plans once they're born?"

Leaning back, she took a moment to really look at his face. The slow muscle working in his jaw. "I don't have a lot of plans. I'm just taking life a second at a time. Trying to savor every step along the way. I'm afraid if I start really laying things out, I'll live for the future, instead of treasuring today." She struggled to find the words, but couldn't. "I don't know how to explain it, exactly."

"I think I understand. Maybe I should learn to be a little more spontaneous. My days do kind of run together."

Something funny settled in her tummy. "And right now? Right here? Is this running together?"

"No. I'm painfully aware of each tiny second ticking down."

"You are? Why?" She held her breath.

"Because…I don't want it to end." The words were so soft she had to strain to hear them.

When she realized exactly what he'd said, the air whooshed from her lungs in a big gulp, the puff of mist she caused obscuring her vision for a moment. She realized she didn't want it to end either.

In love.

The very thing she'd been avoiding—trying not to think about—seemed to be written in the sky in bold green ink. Oh, Lord. Could he have feelings for her, too? Was that what he meant by not wanting it to end?

Or was he simply talking about the lights in the sky?

She was afraid to ask—afraid she'd be very wrong.

He'd mentioned marriage at one time, and she'd dismissed it out of hand, not wanting a workaholic

partner helping her raise two children. Not wanting the disappointment when he missed important
milestones in their lives. Worse, she didn't want
those same children growing up believing Greg's
way of living was the right way.

But he was here with her right now, not at work—
something she could have sworn was impossible a
mere month ago. He'd even admitted that he hadn't
been to this house in ages.

So why now?

"About the kids," he said. "I know we really
haven't gotten a chance to talk about the partic-
ulars, and it's still early, but I'd like to help with
them in some way."

In some way. "In what way, exactly?"

"Maybe I could… Well, if they're boys, I could
take them to a hockey game or something. Teach
them how to ride bikes."

"Maybe girls would like to ride bikes and watch
hockey, as well."

"I know. I didn't mean it like that, I just meant…"

Her heart sloshed around in her chest, a gooey
mass of emotion. "I know what you mean, and
it's sweet. Yes, of course you can take them to a
game, just don't—" she searched around for a tact-

ful way to say it "—make promises you can't or won't keep."

"I know I work too much." He sighed. "I've been thinking about cutting back, I just haven't been able to find the right moment."

She licked her lips, knowing it was selfish of her to even ask. "Maybe this is that moment."

He looked at her then reached up to brush her hair off her forehead. "Maybe it is. Maybe I just needed to find a good enough reason." His throat moved as he swallowed. "Hannah, I—"

Something tinkled from inside the house, threatening to break the spell, but Greg waved it away. "It's the house phone. Let it ring. If it's important, my service knows to call my cell."

"Are you sure?"

"I am. For the first time in my life." His head came down, and his lips covered hers in a gentle kiss that was worlds away from that first desperate kiss at the clinic. This was a kind of slow exploration of dormant emotions, as if he was trying to figure out exactly what was happening between them.

She already knew, and it scared her spitless.

What Hannah needed was to figure out what to do with her newfound knowledge. Did she take a chance on Greg, knowing he could break her heart into a million pieces? Or did she back away and never give him the chance to hurt her or the precious lives she carried inside her?

But he'd ignored the phone. Had hinted that she might be the reason he was thinking about cutting back on work. And his kiss certainly didn't feel distracted, as if he was keeping one ear tuned for the ringing to begin again.

No, he was kissing her as if he wanted more.

As if he never wanted this moment to end. Those words, the ones he'd used earlier, sealed her decision, and she began kissing him back. Eagerly, allowing her own pent-up emotions to surge to the surface.

Her hands reached for him, bringing him even closer.

Greg groaned against her mouth. "I just wanted to talk. I swear. But I can't think straight when you're around."

She smiled. "Join the club. Sometimes there's a time to talk and sometimes there's a time to…do other things."

"Is this one of those times?"

"Oh, I think so. Don't you?" Her heart swelled

with love. Talking could definitely wait. They had all day tomorrow to figure the other stuff out.

Greg dragged her to her feet, still kissing her. In a second he'd scooped her up in his arms. "We'll have to go to my room. My parents' room…"

She laughed. "It's okay. I'm sure they'd appreciate it if they knew."

"I think they already might. When I called to ask about the keys, my mom's voice turned kind of hopeful."

"What did you tell her?" She wasn't talking about the twins exactly, she doubted Greg would have mentioned the pregnancy to his mom.

"That I wanted to bring a friend up here to talk."

"Does she know what happens when you try to do that?" She nipped his chin. "All kinds of naughty things."

He gave a mock shudder. "Let's not use the words *mom* and *naughty* in the same conversation."

"Fine by me."

He carried her into the house, and Hannah gave the lights in the distance one last look, noticing the brilliant colors were just beginning to fade, as if they knew there was no longer anyone to witness their display.

Greg kicked the front door shut behind him, and

the warmth of the interior of the house washed over her. Halfway down the hall, the phone rang again, but this time the sound was different. This one carried ominous undertones.

A trickle of fear went through her when Greg stopped dead. "What is it? Is that your cell?"

"I programmed a different ring tone for the hospital's number."

She stiffened. "Put me down. You have to answer it."

He did as she asked, striding to the credenza in the foyer and glancing at the screen as he picked up the cell. "Hello?"

His expression quickly darkened, until it matched the fear that had filtered through her a moment earlier. Something was terribly wrong.

Within a few seconds she had her answer. "I'll be there as soon as I can, but I'm an hour and a half out. Call Dr. Calhoun to handle it until I arrive." He clicked a button on the phone and then dragged a hand through his hair, a soft curse erupting from his lips.

The same ones that had kissed her a minute ago. "What is it?"

"We have to leave. It's Claire Taylor." He wheeled

around grabbing his keys. "Perforated appendix. It's spewed bacteria into her abdominal cavity."

"Oh, God." For someone with an immune system already weakened from chemotherapy, a burst appendix could be catastrophic. "Let's go."

She paused just long enough to scoop up her purse and her coat. Greg waited, but didn't say a word.

Neither did he talk the whole agonizing way home. Hannah tried to boost his optimism with little anecdotes about other chemo patients who'd suffered massive infections and lived. Claire could be one of those.

She had to be. Because if she wasn't…

Hannah didn't want to go there. Instead, she thought about Claire's bubbly personality, which had persisted even while sick. Her excitement about starting the breast reconstruction process.

She'd be okay. Maybe it wasn't as bad as Greg thought. Maybe the appendix hadn't actually burst. But she knew that chemotherapy could mask the symptoms of appendicitis. The body's immune system wasn't strong enough to mount a good attack on the infection, which was where the pain from appendicitis often arose. So Claire might not have even known something was seriously wrong until it was…

No. It wasn't too late. It couldn't be.

The outcome would have been the same no matter where she and Greg were.

Something crossed her mind. If they hadn't been together at the cabin, one of them would have still been in Anchorage to get that call. One of them would have been within a stone's throw of the hospital.

Only they'd both been out of the area. And because of it, a woman's life could be in danger. The house phone had rung. They'd ignored it, figuring it wasn't anything work related. But would the ten-minute lapse from one phone to the other really make that much of a difference? Who knew?

The hospital had other doctors. Brilliant ones, like Dr. Calhoun. Professionals who were every bit as capable as Greg. He couldn't carry the weight of every single patient on his broad shoulders.

But wasn't she carrying some of it? She was riddled with guilt over not being in Anchorage, and she wasn't even Claire's primary doctor. The buck didn't stop with her. It stopped with Greg.

And from the tight, closed expression on his face, the whitened knuckles as he gripped the steering-wheel, he knew that all too well. If something happened to Claire, he'd never forgive himself for coming away to the cabin.

And because of her part in it, neither would she.

CHAPTER NINETEEN

SHE made him miserable.

Just like his sister said he'd be if he tried to become someone he wasn't. Like a commercial fisherman. Or a family man.

Claire was in Intensive Care, fighting for her life, and although Greg had come out a couple of times and squeezed Hannah's hand, she could see it in his face. The abject misery. The hopelessness.

If it wasn't for her, they both knew he'd have been in Anchorage to receive that call. He'd have never gone to that cabin by himself. He'd done it for her. Trying to be someone he wasn't.

In fact, he'd talked about needing a good enough reason to cut back on his patients, patients that were as important to him—no, *more* important— as eating or breathing. At the time she'd been thrilled, hoping she might be that reason.

And now he was paying the price. Would continue to pay the price each time he looked at her or the twins. How long before he couldn't stand it anymore?

Hannah had known who he was from the very beginning and yet time and time again she'd asked him for more. And when he tried to give it, she'd begin her trek up the mountain of hope, only to slip back down the icy slope as soon as she neared the summit.

She didn't want him to have to choose between being with her and doing his job. Didn't want him to give up something he'd devoted his entire life to. And he would. Whether it was out of responsibility or because he loved her, the outcome would be the same.

He'd be miserable. For the rest of his life.

She leaned against the wall, closing her eyes for a few minutes as she tried to come up with some kind of solution, but her mind kept leading her back to the same place over and over. Even here at the hospital Greg had been torn between his patient and Hannah, as evidenced by him having to leave his post to bring her news.

There was no flicker of relief when his eyes met hers, only a deep-seated guilt that might never go away.

Unless she did.

The whispered words slid through her mind so quickly she almost missed them—had to call them back.

Unless she did.

The terrible ripping sensation inside her had nothing to do with the babies and everything to do with the pain that sometimes came from doing the right thing.

And it was. If she went away, Greg could go back to the life he was meant to have. He'd never have to face choosing between her and his job. He'd never sit at home when he wanted to be at the clinic. Never feel that spark of love slowly turn to hate as the years rolled by.

And the babies?

No. She never wanted them to wonder if they were the cause of their father's unhappiness.

Hot tears spilled from her eyes, coursing down her cheeks. She scrubbed them away but more followed, until there was an endless river. Oh, God. She didn't want him to see her like this. Didn't want to give him one more thing to feel guilty about.

Before she could talk herself out of it, she moved away from her perch near the double doors of the emergency room and stepped onto the pad that caused them to swish open. Then, putting one foot in front of the other, she walked away into the night.

Where was she?

Two weeks and no word from Hannah. He'd gone back to the emergency room for the fifth time, only to find her gone. The fight for Claire's life had consumed most of his time and had kept him from really searching the hospital. He'd assumed she'd gone home, knowing she couldn't do anything more for him or their patient, but never in his wildest nightmares had he imagined her walking away from him. From the clinic.

He fingered the note he'd found on his desk the day after the emergency.

Sorry. I can't do this anymore. I'll let you know when they're born. Hannah

He closed his eyes as the pain squeezed around his heart again. She couldn't do what? Spend one more day with someone who was married to his job? Couldn't watch any more patients suffer? Couldn't bear the constant reminders of what she'd once lived through?

After two weeks he was no closer to deciphering the meaning behind those words than when he'd arrived at his office that Sunday night and found the neatly folded piece of paper. He'd stared at it uncomprehendingly for several puzzled moments before he'd realized it meant goodbye. And not just for a week or two.

Forever.

He'd contacted Dr. Preston but she hadn't heard from Hannah, and even if she had, she couldn't tell him where she was.

Stella had pulled Hannah's personnel file for him. It was still splayed open on his desk. The phone number for the house in Anchorage was there, as was the address. He'd swung by to find her things were still there, as was her car, but there'd been no sign of Hannah's vibrant presence. Instead, the place was dark and empty, as if she'd disappeared off the face of the earth.

She hadn't. He even had a pretty good idea of where she might have gone.

Idaho.

There was an emergency phone number and address listed but until he could figure out the meaning of her note, he wasn't going anywhere.

Maybe she'd be back.

His fingers trailed across the indentation of her handwriting, the paper cold and lifeless under his skin. She wouldn't be back. Not unless he went and got her.

But if she didn't want to be here?

Damn.

A knock sounded at the door. For a second his hopes leaped, only to crash again when Stella's voice came from the other side. "Greg?"

"Come in." He flipped the note over, not wanting her to see what a colossal fool he was for wanting a woman he couldn't have.

She stalked through the door, holding a sheet of paper and waving it at him. "Can I ask what you're doing?"

"What do you mean?" He tilted his head, trying to see exactly what she was so riled up about. The schedule?

"I thought you told her you were going to slow down."

He realized what she was talking about and bristled. "Hannah's not here anymore, so it's business as usual. You don't have to stay past six o'clock. I've already told you."

"She quit, didn't she?"

"You know as much as I do."

Her eyes went to the desk and landed on the sheet of paper his hand still rested on. She gave a knowing grunt. "I don't know what you did, but Hannah loved it here."

His jaw tightened. "Not enough to stick around, evidently."

"Does her leaving have anything to do with Claire Taylor?"

Claire. The woman who reminded him so much of Bethany. And she was better, the surgery and antibiotics had worked their magic.

Surely Hannah didn't blame him for leaving the cabin early to treat the woman? He could have sworn Hannah cared for Claire, as well. But what else could the "I can't do this anymore" mean, other than she was tired of his work pulling him one way and then the other?

But it pulled her, as well. She'd left her house to come and help him with the computer on her day off, had knitted hats in her spare time for patients—in fact, there was an unopened one on the coffee table right now—so wasn't it a little hypocritical of her to be miffed about their time together being cut short?

Greg looked up at Stella. "I don't know. Maybe."

"Did you ever think maybe she cares about you?"

If so, why did she leave, just as he was acknowledging his own feelings for her?

He shrugged. "It doesn't really matter at this point, does it?"

She sucked down a deep audible breath, her exasperation obvious. "You two are like stubborn little kids." She nodded at the desk. "You show me yours and I'll show you mine."

"Excuse me?" He stared at her, wondering if he'd worked her too hard.

"Your note. You show me yours—" she reached in the pocket of her scrubs and pulled out a slip of paper "—and I'll show you mine."

"Where did you get that?" He'd torn the office apart, looking for any other notes she might have left. He could have sworn there'd been none.

"Remember the computer that goes on the fritz periodically? It wouldn't start up on Monday morning so I reached down to wiggle the cord, and there it was. She knew I'd find it." Stella unfolded the note while she continued to talk. "You never got that computer fixed. Just like you never fixed whatever was wrong with you."

"What was wrong with…" He frowned. "What are you talking about?"

She glanced down at the paper and began to read. "'Stella, I'm so sorry to leave you in the lurch, but I can't stay. I'd just end up making him unhappy if I do. Please make sure he eats. But above all, don't let him kill himself.'" She looked up again and met his eyes. "'My love to you and the rest of the staff. Hannah.'"

He swallowed hard. *I'd just end up making him unhappy.* Was that what she really thought? Hell, he couldn't remember a time he'd ever been *more* unhappy than these past two weeks.

"Do you know where she went?"

Stella shrugged. "I imagine she's gone home to Idaho."

Exactly what he'd thought. "Her car is still in her driveway."

"So you did go over there. I wondered." She glanced again at his desk. "What did yours say?"

A hell of a lot less than hers did. He flipped the note over and turned it so Stella could read it.

She nodded as if she understood exactly what the words meant. "And that bag?"

He glanced at the coffee table where the gift bag sat. "Hannah's been knitting hats for the patients." He hadn't been able to bear to look inside it.

"Who's it for?"

"I don't know. There's no tag."

That was strange. Hannah had tagged each of the gifts, just like Martha Brookstone had done.

Stella went over to the table and undid the tie that held the decorative rope handles together. She pulled a brown hat from the interior of the bag. Greg couldn't even look at the thing. Hannah had turned her back on him and walked away without a single word of explanation—other than a damn note that said nothing at all. Suddenly furious, he crumpled the paper in his fist and chucked it into the basket that sat beside his hideous desk.

He vaguely heard Stella gasp and turn toward him.

Alarmed, he stood. "What is it?"

She brought the hat over to the desk. There hadn't been a tag on the package but there was one dangling from the item itself. This hat wasn't all fluffy like the others, with floaty little strings that danced when you walked. This was a sensible woolen affair made of dark brown yarn with some kind of beige diamond pattern running through it.

Stella handed it to him. "Read it."

He didn't want to touch it but as she'd thrust it into his hands, he didn't have much choice. Turning the little tag with a flick of his finger, the same handwriting that had been on the note came into view. *Everyone should have a special hat. I was worried you might be cold.*

When he looked back up, he noted that his normally stoic receptionist's eyes were suspiciously moist.

"I don't understand."

"Of course you don't." Stella sniffed. "She made it for you, you knucklehead."

He turned the hat over and over in his hands, still not comprehending. She'd made several hats for different people. Then he remembered telling Annie, his young patient, that he didn't have a special hat to keep him warm—Hannah had been in the room at the time.

She'd made him one. The special hat he'd said he didn't have.

Suddenly it didn't matter that he didn't understand why she'd done it. And it wasn't going to do him a lick of good to keep sitting here brooding about why she'd left. The fact that she'd mentioned letting him know when the babies were born was telling. She didn't mean to cut him out of her life entirely. She certainly could have made that note a lot harsher and a lot more final: *don't bother contacting me again.* Instead, she'd left him a hat—a little piece of herself—worried he might get cold at some point.

"Stella, what does our schedule look like this week?"

She raised her brows. "Exactly like it did before Hannah came into our lives, remember?"

And that was the problem. As much as he might try to go back to the way things had been before, it wasn't going to work. Because Hannah *had* come into their lives and nothing would ever be the same again.

"Can you book me a flight?"

Stella smiled. "Now you're talking. For what date?"

"We need to reschedule or refer all our patients. After that, I want the first available flight." He picked up the hat and tucked it under his arm. "Oh, and somewhere in my paperwork is the number for the storage unit where my old desk is. See if you can get them to bring it back here, will you? And donate this one to charity."

Hannah slid her left foot into the stirrup and swung herself into the saddle. Poncho nickered and tossed his head, ready to get home to his warm stall and the flake of hay that was waiting in his feed crib.

Leaning down, she rubbed the quarterhorse's

neck. "Thanks for the ride, boy. Sorry there aren't any more cows to wrangle."

Her dad's time of working the cows had ended last year when his Parkinson's had begun to affect his time in the saddle. The cattle had been sold off, but her mom kept two of the horses, including Hannah's mount. Now pushing seventeen, the gelding had come a long way from the green-broke four-year-old he'd been when they'd bought him. Hannah had trained him herself as a teenager.

She missed riding. Missed the freedom that came with galloping across the fields after a stray calf or riding the fence line in search of breaks or gaps.

She missed a lot of things.

But most of all she missed Greg.

She put a hand on the slight bump on her abdomen and wondered again if she'd done the right thing in leaving. But how could she have stayed when each day she'd have wondered if he regretted being with her? Regret being tied down to a relationship and kids?

Something in her had hoped he'd come after her and prove her wrong, especially once he realized she'd knitted that hat especially for him. But he hadn't. She'd have to make a decision about her house in Alaska pretty soon. And there was a job in the Boise area that looked promising, at a pediatrician's office.

No more oncology. No more reminders of her past.

She stopped short as a realization struck her. Sometimes you *needed* to face the past in order to tackle the future.

Gathering the reins, she gave Poncho's sides a slight squeeze with her legs and he immediately responded. His walk was a bit more energetic on the way in than it had been on trip here. No need to guide him at this point, he knew the way home by heart.

Her own words came back to her. *Sometimes you need to face the past in order to tackle the future.*

Wasn't that what Greg had done? He hadn't turned his back on the pain of his sister's death. Instead, he'd faced it on a daily basis with every patient he treated. Patients like her, like Martha Brookstone. Patients like Claire Taylor.

How was Claire?

Hannah had flown out of Alaska almost immediately so she had no idea if the woman had recovered or not. She'd left Greg to deal with the situation on his own.

A wave of nausea went through her. She'd taken

the coward's way out. Yes, she'd had Greg's best interests at heart but, thinking back on it, how much easier had it been to simply drop a note on his desk and clear out without ever having to face him?

Too damn easy. Her mom used to say that was a sure sign you were doing the wrong thing.

A sound in the distance brought both her and Poncho's heads up. Her mount gave a whinny of recognition as another horse made its way toward them. It had to be Glenda, her mom's horse. She squinted. The figure on the mare's back was too wide to be her mother. Surely her dad wasn't out here riding. Even the easy, collected canter Glenda was doing would be difficult for him to maintain for more than a couple of strides. And this rider was perfectly at home at the gait, his form flawless.

Poncho tried to break into a trot but Hannah held him back, a feeling of unease rolling over her. What if something had happened to her father?

When the rider was about fifty yards out, Hannah leaned forward, trying to figure out who was in the saddle.

Oh, God. That's why the person looked so familiar.

It was Greg.

On a horse!

She pulled Poncho to a halt, half wondering if she'd gone crazy. Greg didn't know how to ride. He didn't have time to do anything other than work. She didn't want Poncho moving suddenly and spooking Glenda. Except Greg knew his way around a horse. She'd swear it from his posture, the way he held the reins gathered in his left hand while his right rested quietly on his thigh.

He pulled up beside her. "Hi."

"You ride." The inane comment drew a laugh from him.

"I haven't in a long time, and I'm pretty sure I'm going to pay dearly for it tomorrow but, yes. I do. It feels good."

"How's Claire?" Poncho stepped sideways, anxious to be on his way.

"She's almost fully recovered."

Relief washed over her. "That's wonderful."

"That's not why I'm here, though."

She licked her lips. "I kind of figured."

Greg turned his horse so they were head to head. "I came to ask what you meant by your note."

"I, uh…" She shrugged. "I could tell you weren't happy. I decided to make it easy on you."

"Easy on…" Greg swung off Glenda and held his

hands out for Poncho's reins. "I'd rather not have this conversation on horseback."

Hannah didn't have much choice but to follow his lead so she dismounted and let him tie the horses to a nearby bush.

She stood still, not convinced this wasn't all part of some strange hallucination. But when he came back and she realized he was wearing her father's broken-down cowboy boots, she knew he was very real. In Idaho. Riding her mother's horse.

"You decided to make it easy on me?"

"Yes."

He took two steps forward and wrapped his arms around her, holding her tight against him. His scent washed over her, clean, earthy and smelling like horse, and she couldn't keep herself from leaning into him.

When he spoke, his voice was low. "If this was easy, I don't ever want to face hard." He paused. "I love you, Hannah. What on earth gave you the idea I was unhappy?"

Her heart flipped over in her chest. He loved her? Surely she hadn't heard that correctly. "I—I didn't want you to have to choose between me and your job."

He kissed the top of her head. "That choice was already made."

"But you looked miserable at the hospital."

Greg's hand slid through her hair. "I'm upset any time there's a problem with one of my patients. You saw what happened with Mrs. Brookstone."

"Yes." Although it made her sad that it had taken the woman's illness to bring them together, she thought Martha would be pleased if she could see them now. "But you didn't want a wife or children. You said as much."

He chuckled. "I did. Stupid people say stupid things sometimes." Holding her away from him, he looked into her face. "My life was so wrapped up with my work that I didn't think I had anything to offer anyone else. But I've realized that without you I don't have much to offer to *anyone*…not even my patients. My heart wouldn't be in it anymore."

"But your sister—"

"Would approve. All she ever wanted was for me to follow my heart. And my heart is here. With you."

Hannah sighed, believing at last. "I love you, too. Are you sure you can do this?"

He cupped her face. "For the past two weeks I've

found out what I *can't* do. And that's live without you. I think Stella agrees with me."

"She found my note?"

"Yes. And she opened your present—which I hadn't been able to do." He pulled the hat from his back pocket. "Thank you for worrying. It gave me the nerve to finally come after you."

"I'm so very glad you did."

He leaned in for a long kiss. The parts of her that had gone into hibernation slowly came back to life. When he pulled away, he leaned his forehead against hers, one hand curving over her abdomen. "Will you come back to Alaska with me?"

"Yes, but first I have a better idea." She took him by the hand and led him toward the horses. "My folks have a little cottage that sits about a hundred yards from the main house. It's where the ranch foreman used to stay. I don't think they'll miss us if we spend an hour or so over there. We can sneak in through one of the back windows."

He laughed. "I don't think we'll need to use the window."

"Really? And why's that?"

He lifted his hand, something shiny dangling from his index finger. "Your mom gave me a key to the front door."

EPILOGUE

HANNAH stood over the crib and watched the twins sleep.

Simon and Bethany huddled at opposite ends of the space, still looking incredibly tiny, although at a little over five pounds each they were good-sized. "It's almost time, munchkins."

She held a sealed envelope in a shaking hand, wondering what news it contained.

Greg loved these little ones as much as she did, doted on them every second that he was home, which was a lot more often than she expected. He didn't seem to be able to stay away for longer than six hours at a time.

In fact, they'd bought a house closer to the clinic so Greg could come home for lunch or whenever there was a lull between patients. And it was also close enough to the hospital that she didn't worry about keeping him away from anything urgent.

"And he's not miserable after all," she whispered to the babies.

Neither was she. In fact, Hannah was insanely happy. She'd go back to work in another month, and the timing was perfect. Fishing season would be over, and Greg's parents had offered to come up and help out. Between the heart-to-heart talk Greg and his father had finally had and the birth of the twins, the hard feelings between the two men had been eased. They were both stubborn and prideful, but Bethany's memory would serve as a permanent link between them. Greg's mother was a sweet woman, and Hannah knew the twins would be in good hands with both of them.

The front door clicked shut. "Hannah? I'm home."

Greg's voice reverberated around the house, and she winced when one set of eyes opened and then the other.

Awake. Again.

She smiled. It was all good. Sneaking from the nursery and hoping to get a few minutes alone with her husband, she padded out to the front room.

Greg caught her around the waist and pulled her against his body before kissing her breathless. After six months of marriage he still held her like he couldn't get enough.

And that was fine by her because she couldn't get enough of him either.

Once she caught his eye, she held up the envelope. "The results are in."

His smile faded as he looked at her hand. "Did you open it?"

"No. I wanted to wait for you to get home. I think we should do it together."

He brushed a long strand of hair behind her shoulder. Over the course of her pregnancy her hair had grown six inches and was shiny and healthy again. Just like she felt.

A thin cry from one of the twins went up.

"Oh, no. They were stirring when you got home but I was hoping they'd go right back to sleep."

"It's Bethany, I'll get her."

Hannah was amazed that he could tell their cries apart so easily, but he could. Thirty seconds later he strolled out of the room, a baby snuggled in his arms. Wide blue eyes stared up at her daddy and little fists waved from beneath her blanket. Hannah smiled then went over to the couch and waited for him to join her. He did, kissing his daughter's forehead as he sat.

He stared at Bethany for a long time then looked

up at her. "It doesn't matter, you know. It won't change anything."

"Don't you want to know one way or the other?"

"Not really. Unless you do."

Hannah frowned, not sure where this sudden reluctance had come from. Was he afraid the twins weren't his? Was he afraid he wouldn't feel the same way about them?

"I'm their father. It doesn't matter whose D.N.A. they carry." He took the envelope from her hand and set it unopened on the coffee table. "We'll keep it in a file somewhere, in case they need or want to know someday. But I'm okay with never opening it."

"Are you sure?"

Securing Bethany in one arm, he reached for her with the other, sliding his hand beneath her hair and pulling her close. "As sure as I am that I love you," he whispered.

A wave of happiness burst over her as his lips touched hers, and Hannah knew without a doubt this was where she belonged. In the arms of the man whose love stretched as far and wide as the northern lights across a dark Alaskan sky.

* * * * *

Mills & Boon® Large Print
Medical

July

THE SURGEON'S DOORSTEP BABY	Marion Lennox
DARE SHE DREAM OF FOREVER?	Lucy Clark
CRAVING HER SOLDIER'S TOUCH	Wendy S. Marcus
SECRETS OF A SHY SOCIALITE	Wendy S. Marcus
BREAKING THE PLAYBOY'S RULES	Emily Forbes
HOT-SHOT DOC COMES TO TOWN	Susan Carlisle

August

THE BROODING DOC'S REDEMPTION	Kate Hardy
AN INESCAPABLE TEMPTATION	Scarlet Wilson
REVEALING THE REAL DR ROBINSON	Dianne Drake
THE REBEL AND MISS JONES	Annie Claydon
THE SON THAT CHANGED HIS LIFE	Jennifer Taylor
SWALLOWBROOK'S WEDDING OF THE YEAR	Abigail Gordon

September

NYC ANGELS: REDEEMING THE PLAYBOY	Carol Marinelli
NYC ANGELS: HEIRESS'S BABY SCANDAL	Janice Lynn
ST PIRAN'S: THE WEDDING!	Alison Roberts
SYDNEY HARBOUR HOSPITAL: EVIE'S BOMBSHELL	Amy Andrews
THE PRINCE WHO CHARMED HER	Fiona McArthur
HIS HIDDEN AMERICAN BEAUTY	Connie Cox